IRISH SHORT STORIES

Irish Short Stories

SEAMUS O'KELLY

Author of
THE WEAVER'S GRAVE

THE MERCIER PRESS
4 BRIDGE STREET, CORK

© *The Mercier Press*

Reprinted 1969
Reprinted 1973
Reprinted 1976

SBN 85342 141 2

Contents

I   The Can with the Diamond Notch . . .   7

II   Both Sides of the Pond 30

III   The White Goat 42

IV   Michael and Mary 52

V   The Haven 59

VI   The Man with the Gift 70

VII   A Wayside Burial 83

The Can with the Diamond Notch

Festus Clasby, the name stood out in chaste white letters from the black background of the signboard. Indeed the name might be said to spring from the landscape, for this shop jumped from its rural setting with an air of aggression. It was a commercial oasis on a desert of grass. It proclaimed the clash of two civilisations. There were the hills, pitched round it like the galleries of some vast amphitheatre, rising tier upon tier to the blue of the sky. There was the yellow road, fantastic in its frolic down to the valley. And at one of its wayward curves was the shop, the shop of Festus Clasby, a foreign growth upon the landscape, its one long window crowded with sombre merchandise, its air that of established, cob-web respectability.

Inside the shop was Festus Clasby himself, like some great masterpiece in its ancient frame. He was the product of the two civilizations, a charioteer who drove the two fiery steeds of Agricolo and Trade with a hand of authority. He was a man of lands and of shops. His dark face, framed in darker hair and beard, was massive and square. Behind the luxurious growth of hair the rich blood glowed on the clear skin. His chest had breadth, his limbs were great, showing girth at the hips and power at the calves. His eyes were large and dark, smouldering in soft velvety tones. The nose was long, the nostrils expressive of a certain animalism, the mouth looked eloquent.

His voice was low, of an agreeable even quality, floating over the boxes and barrels of his shop like a chant. His words never jarred, his views were vaguely comforting, based on accepted conventions, expressed in round, soft, lulling platitudes. His manner was serious, his movements deliberate, the great bulk of the shoulders looming up in unconscious but dramatic poses in the curiously uneven lighting of the shop. His hands gave the impression of slowness and a moderate skill; they could make up a parcel on the counter without leaving ugly laps; they could perform a minor surgical operation on a beast in the fields without degenerating to butchery; and they would always be doing something, even if it were only rolling up a ball of twine. His clothes exuded a faint suggestion of cinnamon, nutmeg and caraway seeds.

Festus Clasby would have looked the part in any notorious position in life; his shoulders would have carried with dignity the golden chain of office of the mayoralty of a considerable city; he would have looked a perfect chairman of a jury at a Coroner's inquest; as the Head of a pious Guild in a church he might almost be confused with the figures of the stained glass windows; marching at the head of a brass band he would have reconciled one to death. There was no technical trust which men would not have reposed in him, so perfectly was he wrought as a human casket. As it was Festus Clasby filled the most fatal of all occupations to dignity without losing his tremendous illusion of respectability. The hands which cut the bacon and the tobacco turned the taps over pint measures, scooped bran and flour into scales,

8

took herrings out of their barrels, rolled up sugarsticks in shreds of paper for children, were hands whose movements the eyes of no saucy customer dared follow with a gleam of suspicion. Not once in a lifetime was that casket tarnished; the nearest he ever went to it was when he bought up very cheaply as was his custom – a broken man's insurance policy a day after the law made such a practice illegal. There was no haggling at Festus Clasby's counter. There was only conversation, agreeable conversation about things which Festus Clasby did not sell, such as the weather, the diseases of animals, the results of races, and the scandals of the Royal Families of Europe. These conversations were not hurried or yet protracted. They came to a happy ending at much the same moment as Festus Clasby made the knot on the twine of your parcel. But to stand in the devotional light in front of his counter, wedged in between divisions and sub-divisions of his boxes and barrels, and to scent the good scents which exhaled from his shelves, and to get served by Festus Clasby in person, was to feel that you had been indeed served.

The small farmers and herds and the hardy little dark mountainy men had this reverential feeling about the good man and his shop. They approached the establishment as holy pilgrims might approach a shrine. They stood at his counter with the air of devotees. Festus Clasby waited on them with patience and benignity. He might be some warm-blooded god handing gifts out over the counter. When he brought forth his great account book and entered up their purchases with a carpenter's pencil – having first moistened the

9

tip of it with his flexible lips – they had strongly, deep down in their souls, the conviction that they were then and for all time debtors to Festus Clasby. Which, indeed and in truth, they were. From year's end to year's end their accounts remained in that book; in the course of their lives various figures rose and faded after their names, recording the ups and downs of their financial histories. It was only when Festus Clasby had supplied the materials for their wakes that the great pencil, with one mighty stroke of terrible finality, ran like a sword through their names, wiping their very memories from the hillsides. All purchases were entered up in Festus Clasby's mighty record without vulgar discussions as to price. The business of the establishment was conducted on the basis of a belief in the man who purchased. The customers of Festus Clasby would as soon have thought of questioning his prices as they would of questioning the right of the earth to revolve round the sun. Festus Clasby was the planet around which this constellation of small farmers, herds, and hardy little dark mountainy men revolved; from his shop they drew the light and heat and food which kept them going. Their very emotions were registered at his counter. To the man with a religious turn he was able at a price to hand down from his shelves the *Key of Heaven*; the other side of the box he comforted the man who came panting to his taps to drown the memory of some chronic impertinence. He gave a very long credit, and a very long credit, in his philosophy, justified a very, very long profit. As to security, if Festus Clasby's customers had not a great deal of money they had grass which grew every year, and the beasts which Festus Clasby fattened and sold at the fairs had sometimes to eat his debtors out of his book. If his bullocks were not able to do even this, then Festus Clasby talked to the small farmer about a mortgage on the land, so that now and again small farmers became herds for Festus Clasby. In this way was he able to maintain his position with his back to the hills and his toes in the valley, striding his territory like a Colossus. When you saw his name on the signboard standing stark from the landscape, and when you saw Festus Clasby behind his counter, you knew instinctively that both had always stood for at least twenty shillings in the pound.

2

Now, it came to pass that on a certain day Festus Clasby was passing through the outskirts of the nearest country town on his homeward journey, his cart laden with provisions. At the same moment the spare figure of a tinker whose name was Mac-an-Ward, the Son of the Bard, veered around the corner of a street with a new tin can under his arm. It was the Can with the Diamond Notch.

Mac-an-Ward approached Festus Clasby, who pulled up his cart. 'Well, my good man?' queried Festus Clasby, a phrase usually addressed across his counter, his hands outspread, to longstanding customers.

'The last of a rare lot,' said Mac-an-Ward, deftly poising the tin can on the top of his fingers, so that it stood level with Festus Clasby's great face. Festus

Clasby took this as a business proposition, and the soul of the trader revolved within him. Why not buy the tin can from this tinker and sell it at a profit across his counter, even as he would sell the flitches of bacon that were wrapped in sacking upon his cart? He was in mellow mood, and laid down the reins in the cart beside him.

'And so she is the last?' he said, eyeing the tin can.

'She is the Can with the Diamond Notch.'

'Odds and ends go cheap,' said Festus Clasby.

'She is the last, but the flower of the flock.'

'Remnants must go as bargains or else remain as remnants.'

'My wallet!' protested Mac-an-Ward, 'you wound me Don't speak as if I picked it off a scrap heap.'

'I will not but I will say that being a tail end and an odd one it must go at a sacrifice.'

The Son of the Bard tapped the side of the can gently with his knuckles.

'Listen to him, the hard man from the country! He has no regard for my feelings. I had the soldering iron in my hand in face of it before the larks stirred this morning. I had my back to the East, but through the bottom of that can there I saw the sun rise in its glory. The brightness of it is as the harvest moon.'

'I don't want it for its brightness.'

'Dear heart, listen to the man who would not have brightness. He would pluck the light from the moon, quench the heat in the heart of the sun. He would draw a screen across the aurora borealis and paint out the rainbow with lamp black. He might do such things, but he cannot deny the brightness of this can. Look upon

12

it! When the world is coming to an end it will shine up at the sky and it will say! "Ah, where are all the great stars now that made a boast of their brightness?" And there will be no star left to answer. They will all be dead things in the heaven buried in the forgotten graves of the skies.'

'Don't mind the skies. Let me see if there may not be a leakage in it.' Festus Clasby held up the can between his handsome face and the bright sky.

'Leakages!' exclaimed Mac-an-Ward.

'A leakage in a can that I soldered as if with my own heart's blood. Holy Kilcock, what a mind has this man from the country! He sees no value in its brightness; now he will tell me that there is no virtue in its music.'

'I like music,' said Festus Clasby. 'No fiddler has ever stood at my door but had the good word to say of me. Not one of them could ever say that he went thirsty from my counter.'

Said the Son of the Bard: 'Fiddlers, what are fiddlers? What sound have they like the music of the sweet milk going into that can from the yellow teats of the red cow? Morning and evening there will be a hymn played upon it in the haggard. Was not the finest song ever made called *Cailin deas cruidhte na mbo*? Music! Do you think that the water in the holy well will not improve in its sparkle to have such a can as this dipped into it? It will be welcome everywhere for its clearness and its cleanness. Heavenly Father, look at the manner in which I rounded the edge of that can with the clippers! Cut clean and clever, soldered at the dawn of day, the dew falling upon the hands that moulded it, the parings scattered about my feet like jewels. And now you would bargain over it. I will not sell it to you at all. I will put it in a holy shrine.'

Festus Clasby turned the can over in his hands, a little bewildered. 'It looks an ordinary can enough,' he said.

'It is the Can with the Diamond Notch,' declared Mac-an-Ward.

'Would it be worth a shilling now?'

'He puts a price upon it! It is blasphemy. The man has no religion; he will lose his soul. The devils will have him by the heels. They will tear his red soul through the roof. Give me the can; don't hold it in those hands any longer. They are coarse; the hair is standing about the purple knuckles like stubbles in an ill-cut meadow. That can was made for the hands of a delicate woman or for the angels that carry water to the Court of Heaven. I saw it in a vision the night before I made it; it was on the head of a maiden with golden hair. Her feet were bare and like shells. She walked across a field where daisies rose out of young grass; she had the can resting on her head like one coming from the milking. So I rose up then and said, "Now, I will make a can fit for this maiden's head." And I made it out of the rising sun and the falling dew. And now you ask me if it is worth a shilling.'

'For all your talk, it is only made of tin, and not such good tin.'

'Not good tin! I held it in my hand in the piece before ever the clippers was laid upon it. I bent it and it curved, supple as a young snake. I shook it, and the ripples ran down the length of it like silver waves in a little lake. The strength of the ages was in its voice. It has gathered its power in the womb of the earth. It was smelted from the precious metal taken from the mines of the Peninsula of Malacca, and it will have its gleam when the sparkle of the diamond is spent.'

'I'll give you a shilling for it, and hold your tongue.'

'No! I will not have it on my conscience. God is my judge, I will break it up first. I will cut it into pieces. From one of them will yet be made a breastplate, and in time to come it will be nailed to your own coffin, with your name and your age and the date of your death painted upon it. And when the paint is faded it will shine over the dust of the bone of your breast. It will be dug up and preserved when all graveyards are abolished. They will say, "We will keep this breastplate, for who knows but that it bore the name of the man who refused to buy the Can with the Diamond Notch." '

'How much will you take for it?'

'Now you are respectful. Let me put a price upon it, for it was I who fashioned it into this shape. It will hold three gallons and a half from now until the time that swallows wear shoes. But for all that I will part with it, because I am poor and hungry and have a delicate wife. It breaks my heart to say it but pay into my hands two shillings and it is yours. Pay quickly or I may repent. It galls me to part with; in your charity pay quickly and begone.'

'I will not. I will give you one-and-six.'

'Assassin! You stab me. What a mind you have! Look at the greed of your eyes; they would devour the grass of the fields from this place up to the Devil's Bit. You would lock up the air and sell it in gasping breaths. You are disgusting. But give me the one-and-six and to Connacht with you! I am damning my soul standing beside you and your cart, smelling its contents. How can a man talk with the smell of fat bacon going between him and the wind? One-and-six and the dew that fell at the making hardly dry upon my hands yet. Farewell, a long farewell, my Shining One; we may never meet again.'

The shawl of Mac-an-Ward's wife had been blowing around the nearby corner while this discussion had been in progress. It flapped against the wall in the wind like a loose sail in the rigging. The head of the woman herself came gradually into view, one eye spying around the masonry, half-closing as it measured the comfortable proportions of Festus Clasby seated upon his cart. As the one-and-six was counted out penny by penny into the palm of the brown hand of the Son of the Bard, the figure of his wife floated out on the open road, tossing and tacking and undecided in its direction to the eye of those who understood not the language of gestures and motions. By a series of giddy evolutions she arrived at the cart as the last of the coppers was counted out.

'I have parted with my inheritance,' said Mac-an-Ward. 'I have sold my soul and the angels have folded their wings, weeping.'

'In other words, I have bought a tin can,' said Festus Clasby, and his frame and the entire cart shook with his chuckling.

The tinker's wife chuckled with him in harmony. Then she reached out her hand with a gesture that claimed a sympathetic examination of the purchase.

Festus Clasby hesitated, looking into the eyes of the woman. Was she to be trusted? Her eyes were clear, grey and open, almost babyish in their rounded innocence. Festus Clasby handed her the tin can and she examined it slowly.

'Who sold you the Can with the Diamond Notch?' she asked.

'The man standing by your side.'

'He has wronged you. The can is not his.'

'He says he made it.'

'Liar! He never curved it in the piece.'

'I don't much care whether he did or not. It is mine now anyhow.'

'It is my brother's can. No other hand made it. Look! Do you see this notch on the piece of sheet iron where the handle is fastened to the sides?'

'I do.'

'Is it not shaped like a diamond?'

'It is.'

'By that mark I identify it. My brother cuts that diamond-shaped notch in all the work he puts out from his hands. It is his private mark. The shopkeepers have knowledge of it. There is a value on the cans with that notch shaped like a diamond. This man here makes cans when he is not drunk, but the notch to them is square. The shopkeepers have knowledge of them too for they do not last. The handles fall out of them. He has never given his time to the art, and so does not know how to rivet them.'

'She vilifies me,' said Mac-an-Ward, *sotto voce*.

'Then I am glad he has not sold me one of his own,' said Festus Clasby. 'I have a fancy for the lasting article.'

'You may be able to buy it yet,' said the woman. 'My brother is lying sick of the fever, and I have his right to sell the Can with the Diamond Notch on the handles where they are riveted.'

'But I have bought it already.'

'This man,' said the damsel, in a tone which discounted the husband, 'had no right to sell it. If it is not his property, but the property of my brother, won't you say that he nor no other man has a right to sell it?'

Festus Clasby felt puzzled. He was unaccustomed to dealing with people who raised questions of title. His black brows knit.

'How can a man who doesn't own a thing sell a thing?' she persisted. 'Is it a habit of yours to sell that which you do not own?'

'It is not,' Festus Clasby said, feeling that an assault had been wantonly made on his integrity as a trader. 'No one could ever say that of me. Honest value was ever my motto.'

'And the motto of my brother who is sick with the fever. I will go to him and say, "I met the most respectable-looking man in all Europe, who put a value on your can because of the diamond notch." I will pay into his hands the one-and-six which is its price.'

Festus Clasby had, when taken out of his own peculiar province a heavy mind and the type of mind that will range along side-issues and get lost in them if they are raised often enough and long enough. The diamond notch on the handle, the brother who was sick of the fever, the alleged non-title of Mac-an-Ward, the interposition of the woman, the cans with the handles which fall out, and the cans with the handles which do not fall out, the equity of selling that which does not belong to you – all these things chased each other across Festus Clasby's mind. The Son of the Bard stood silent by the car, looking away down the road with a pensive look on his long, narrow face.

'Pay me the one-and-six to put into the hands of my brother,' the woman said.

Festus Clasby's mind was brought back at once to his pocket. 'No,' he said, 'but this man can give you my money to pay into the hand of your brother.'

'This man,' she said airily, 'has no interest for me. Whatever took place between the two of you in regard to my brother's can I will have nothing to say to.'

'Then if you won't,' said Festus Clasby, 'I will have nothing to do with you. If he had no right to the can you can put the police onto him; that's what police are for.'

'And upon you,' the woman added. 'The police are also for that.'

'Upon me?' Festus Clasby exclaimed, his chest swelling. 'My name has never crossed the mind of a policeman, except, maybe for what he might owe me at the end of the month for pig's heads. I never stood in the shadow of the law. And to this man standing by your side I have nothing to say.'

'You have. You bought from him that which did not belong to him. You received and the receiver is as bad as the rogue. So the law has it. The shadow of the law is great.'

Festus Clasby came down from his car, his face troubled. 'I am not used to this,' he said.

'You are a handsome man, a man thought well of. You have great provisions upon your cart. This man has nothing but the unwashed shirt which hangs on his slack back. It will not become you to march hand-cuffed with his like, going between two policeman to the bridewell.'

'What are you saying of me, woman?'

'It will be no token of business to see your cart and the provisions it contains driven into the yard of the barracks. All the people of this town will see it, for they have many eyes. The people of trade will be coming to their doors, speaking of it. "A man's property was molested," they will say. "What property?" will be asked. "The Can with the Diamond Notch," they will answer; "the man of substance con-spired with the thief to make away with it." These are the words that will be spoken in the streets.'

Festus Clasby set great store on his name, the name he had got painted for the eye of the country over his door.

'I will be known to the police as one extensive in my dealings,' he said.

'They will not couple me with this man who is known as one living outside of the law.'

'It is not for the Peelers to put the honest man on one side and the thief on the other. That will be for the court. You will stand with him upon my charge. The Peelers will say to you, "We know you to be a man of great worth, and the law will uphold you." But the law is slow and a man's good name goes fast.'

Festus Clasby fingered his money in his pocket and the touch of it made him struggle. 'The can may be this man's for all I know. You have no brother and I believe you to be a fraud.'

'That too will be for the law to decide. If I have a brother the law will produce him when his fever is ended. If I have no brother the law will so declare it. If my brother did not make a Can with the Diamond Notch you will know me as one deficient in truth. There is no point under the stars that the law cannot be got to declare upon. But as is right, the law is slow, and will wait for a man to come out of his fever. Before it can decide another man's good name, like a little cloud riding across the sky is gone from the memory of the people and will not come riding back upon the crest of any wind.'

'It will be a great price to be paying for a tin can,' said Festus Clasby. He was turning around with his fingers the coins in his pocket.

The woman put the can on her arm, then covered it up with her shawl, like a hen taking a chick under the protection of her wing.

'I have given you many words,' she said, 'because you are a man sizeable and good to the eye of a foolish woman. If I had not a sick brother I might be induced to let slip his right in the Can with the Diamond Notch for the pleasure I have found in the look of your face. When I saw you on the cart I said, "There is the build of a man which is to my fancy." When I heard your voice I said, "That is good music to the ear of a woman." When I saw your eye I said, "There is danger to the heart of a woman." When I saw your beard I said, "There is great growth from the strength of a man." When you spoke to me and gave me your laugh I said, "Ah, what a place that would be for a woman to be seated, driving the roads of the country on a cart laden with provisions beside one so much to the female liking." But my sick brother waits, and now I go to that which may make away with the goodness of your name. I must seek those who will throw the shadow of the law over many."

She moved away, sighing a quick sigh, as one might who was setting out on a disagreeable mission. Festus Clasby called to her and she came back, her eyes pained as they sought his face. Festus Clasby paid the money, a bright shilling and two threepenny bits, into her hand, wondering vaguely, but virtuously, as he did so, what hardy little dark mountainy man he would later charge up the can to at the double price.

'Now,' said the wife of Mac-an-Ward, putting the money away, 'you have paid me for my brother's can and you would be within your right in getting back your one-and-six from this bad man.' She hitched her shawl contemptuously in the direction of Mac-an-Ward.

Festus Clasby looked at the Son of the Bard with his velvety soft eyes. 'Come, sir,' said he, his tone a little nervous.

Mac-an-Ward hitched his trousers at the hips like a sailor, spat through his teeth, and eyed Festus Clasby through a slit in his half-closed eyes. There was a little patter of the feet on the road on the part of Mac-an-Ward, and Festus Clasby knew enough of the world and its ways to gather that these were scientific movements invented to throw a man in a struggle. He did not like the look of the Son of the Bard.

'I will go home and leave him to God,' he said. 'Hand me the can and I will be shortening my road.'

At this moment three small boys, ragged, eager, their faces hard and weather-beaten, bounded up to the cart. They were breathless and they stood about the woman.'

'Mother!' they cried in chorus. 'The man in the big shop; he is looking for a can.'

'What can?' cried the woman.

The three young voices rose like a great cry: 'The Can with the Diamond Notch.'

The woman caught her face in her hands as if some terrible thing had been said. She stared at the youngsters intently.

'He wants one more to make up an order,' they chanted. 'He says he will pay – '

The woman shrank from them with a cry. 'How much?' she asked.

'Half-a-crown!'

The wife of Mac-an-Ward threw out her arms in a wild gesture of despair. 'My God!' she cried. 'I sold it. I wronged my sick brother.'

'Where did you sell it, mother?'

'Here, to this handsome dark man.'

'How much did he pay?'

'Eighteen-pence.'

The three youngsters raised a long howl, like beagles who had lost their quarry.

Suddenly the woman's face brightened. She looked eagerly at Festus Clasby, then laid the hand of friendship, of appeal, on his arm.

'I have it!' she cried, joyfully.

'Have what?' asked Festus Clasby.

'A way out of the trouble,' she said. 'A means of saving my brother from wrong. A way of bringing him his own for the Can with the Diamond Notch.'

'What way might that be?' asked Festus Clasby, his manner growing sceptical.

'I will go to the shopman with it and get the half-crown. Having got the half-crown I will hurry back here – or you can come with me – and I will pay you back your one-and-six. In that way I will make another shilling and do you no wrong. Is that agreed?'

'It is not agreed,' said Festus Clasby. 'Give me out the tin can, I am done with you now.'

'It's robbery!' cried the woman, her eyes full of a blazing sudden anger.

'What is robbery?' asked Festus Clasby.

'Doing me out of a shilling. Wronging my sick brother out of his earnings. A man worth hundreds, maybe thousands, to stand between a poor woman and a shilling. I am deceived in you.'

'Out with the can,' said Festus Clasby.

'Let the woman earn her shilling,' said Mac-an-Ward His voice came from behind Festus Clasby.

'Our mother must get her shilling,' cried the three youngsters.

Festus Clasby turned about to Mac-an-Ward, and as he did so he noticed that two men had come and set their backs against a wall hard by; they leaned limply, casually, against it, but they were, he noticed, of the same tribe as the Mac-an-Wards.

'It was always lucky, the Can with the Diamond

Notch,' said the woman. 'This offer of the man in the big shop is a sign of it. I will not allow you to break my brother's luck and he lying in his fever.'

'By heaven!' cried Festus Clasby. 'I will have you all arrested. I will have the law on you now.'

He wheeled about the horse and cart, setting his face for the police barrack, which could be seen shining in the distance in the plumage of a magpie. The two men who stood by came over, and from the other side another man and three old women. With Mac-an-Ward, Mrs. Mac-an-Ward, and the three youn Mac-an-Wards, they grouped themselves around Festus Clasby, and he was vaguely conscious that they were grouped with some military art. A low murmur of a dispute arose among them, rising steadily. He could only hear snatches of their words: 'Give it back to him,' 'He won't get it,' 'How can he be travelling without the Can with the Diamond Notch?' 'Is it the Can with the Diamond Notch?' 'No,' 'Maybe it is, maybe it is not,' 'Who knows that?' 'I say yes,' 'Hold your tongue,' 'Be off, you slut,' 'Rattle away.'

People from the town were attracted to the place. Festus Clasby, the dispute stirring something in his own blood, shook his fist in the long narrow face of Mac-an-Ward. As he did so he got a tip on the heels and a pressure upon the chest sent him staggering a few steps back. One of the old women held him up in her arms and another old woman stood before him, striking her breast. Festus Clasby saw the wisps of hair hanging about the bony face and froth on the corners of her mouth. Vaguely he saw the working of the bones of her wasted neck, and below it a long

V-shaped gleam of the yellow tanned breast, which she thumped with her fist. Afterwards the memory of this ugly old trollop remained with him. The youngsters were shooting in and out through the group, sending up unearthly shrieks. Two of the men peeled off their coats and were sparring at each other wickedly, shouting all the time, while Mac-an-Ward was making a tumultuous peace. The commotion and the strife, or the illusion of strife, increased. 'Oh,' an onlooker cried, 'the tinkers are murdering each other!'

The patient horse at last raised its head with a toss and then wheeled about to break away. With the instinct of his kind, Festus Clasby rushed to the animal's head and held him. As he did so the striped petticoats and the tossing shawls of the women flashed about the shafts and the body of the cart. The men raised a hoarse roar.

A neighbour of Festus Clasby driving up the street at this moment, was amazed to see the great man of lands and shops in the midst of the wrangling tinkers. He pulled up, marvelling, then went to him.

'What is this Festus?' he asked.

'They have robbed me,' cried Festus Clasby.

'They have robbed me,' cried Festus Clasby.

'Robbed you?'

'Ay, of money and property.'

'Good God! How much money?'

'I don't rightly know – I forget – some shillings, maybe.'

'Oh! And of property?'

'No matter. It is only one article, but property.'

'Come home, Festus; in the name of God get out of

this,' advised the good neighbour.

But Festus Clasby was strangely moved. He was behaving like a man who had drink taken. Something had happened wounding to his soul. 'I will not go,' he cried. 'I must have back my money.'

The tinkers had now ceased disputing among themselves. They were grouped about the two men as if they were only spectators of an interesting dispute.

'Back I must have my money;' cried Festus Clasby, his great hand going up in a mighty threat. The tinkers clicked their tongues on the roofs of their mouths in a sound of amazement, as much as to say, 'What a terrible thing! What a wonderful and a mighty man!'

'I advise you to come,' persuaded his neighbour.

'Never! God is my judge, never!' cried Festus Clasby.

Again the tinkers clicked their tongues, looked at each other in wonder.

'You will be thankful you brought your life out of this,' said the neighbour. 'Let it not be said of you on the countryside that you were seen wrangling with the tinkers in this town.'

'Shame! Shame! Shame!' broke out like a shocked murmur among the attentive tinkers. Festus Clasby faced his audience in all his splendid proportions. Never was he seen so moved. Never had such a great passion seized him. The soft tones of his eyes were no longer soft. They shone in fiery wrath. 'I will at least have that which I bought twice over!' he cried. 'I will have my tin can!'

Immediately the group of tinkers broke up in the greatest disorder. Hoarse cries broke out among them.

They behaved like people upon whom some fearful doom had been suddenly pronounced. The old women threw themselves about racked with pain and terror. They beat their hands together, threw wild arms in despairing gestures to the sky, raising a harrowing lamentation. The men growled in sullen gutturals. The youngsters knelt on the road, giving out the wild beagle-like howl. Voices cried above the uproar: 'Where is it? Where is the can with the Diamond Notch? Get him the Can with the Diamond Notch! He must have the Can with the Diamond Notch! How can he travel without the Can with the Diamond Notch? He'll die without the Can with the Diamond Notch!'

Festus Clasby was endeavouring to deliver his soul of impassioned protests when his neighbour, assisted by a bystander or two, forcibly hoisted him up on his cart and he was driven away amid a great howling from the tinkers.

It was twilight when he reached his place among the hills, and the good white letters under the thatch showed clear in his eyes. Pulling himself together he drove with an air about the gable and into the wide open yard at the back, fowls clearing out of his way, a sheep-dog coming to welcome him, a mewing mournfully over the half-door of a stable. Festus Clasby was soothed by this homely, this worshipful, environment, and got off the cart with a sigh. Inside the kitchen he could hear the faithful women trotting about preparing the great master's meal. He made ready to carry the provisions into the shop. When he unwrapped the sacking from the bacon, something like a sudden stab went through his breast. Perspiration came out on his forehead. Several large long slices had been cut off in jagged slashes from the flitches. They lay like wounded things on the body of the cart. He pulled down the other purchases feverishly, horror in his face. How many loaves had been torn off his batch of bread? Where were all the packets of tea and sugar, the currants and raisins, the flour, the tobacco, the cream-of-tartar, the caraway seeds, the nutmeg, the lemon peel, the hair oil, the –

Festus Clasby wiped the perspiration from his fore-head. He stumbled out of the yard, sat up on a ditch, and looked across the silent, peaceful, innocent country. How good it was! How lovely were the beasts grazing, fattening, in the fields! His soft velvety eyes were suddenly flooded with a bitter emotion and he wept.

The loaves of bread were under the shawl of the woman who had supported Festus Clasby when he stumbled; the bacon was under another bright shawl; the tobacco and flour fell to the lot of her whose yellow breast showed the play of much sun and many winds; the tea and sugar and the nutmeg and caraway seeds were under the wing of the wife of the Son of the Bard in the Can with the Diamond Notch.

II

Both Sides of the Pond

I

Mrs. Donohoe marked the clearness of the sky, the number and brightness of the stars.

'There will be a share of frost to-night, Denis,' she said.

Denis Donohoe, her son, adjusted a primitive bolt on the stable door, then sniffed at the air, his broad nostrils quivering sensitively as he raised his head.

'There is ice in the wind,' he said.

'Make a start with the turf to the market to-morrow,' his mother advised. 'People in town will be wanting fires now.'

Denis Donohoe walked over to the dim stack of brown turf piled at the back of the stable. It was there since the early fall, the dry earth cut from the bog the turf that would make bright and pleasant fires in the open grates of Connacht for the winter months. Away from it spread the level bogland, a sweep of country that had, they said, in the infancy of the earth been a great oak forest, across which in later times had roved packs of hungry wolves, and which could at this day claim the most primitive form of industry in Western Europe. Out into this bogland in the summer had come from their cabins the peasantry, men and women, Denis Donohoe among them; they had dug up slices of the spongy, wet sod, cut it into pieces rather larger than bricks, licked it into shape by stamping upon it with their bare feet, stacked it about in little rows to dry in the sun, one sod leaning against the other, looking in the moonlight like a great host of wee brown fairies grouped in couples for a midnight dance on the carpet of purple heather. Now the time had come to convert it into such money as it would fetch.

Denis Donohoe whistled merrily that night as he piled the donkey cart, or 'creel', with the sods of turf. Long before daybreak next morning he was about, his movements quick like one who had great business on hands. The kitchen of the cabin was illuminated by a rushlight, the rays of which did not go much beyond a small deal table, scrubbed white, where he sat at his breakfast an unusually good repast, for he had tea, home-made bread and a boiled egg. His mother moved about the dim kitchen, waiting on him, her bare feet almost noiseless on the black earthen floor. He ate heartily and silently, making the Sign of the Cross when he had finished. His mother followed him out on the dark road to bid him good luck, standing beside the creel of turf.

'There should be a brisk demand now that the winter is upon us,' she said hopefully. 'God be with you.'

'God and Mary be with you, mother,' Denis Donohoe made answer as he took the donkey by the head and led him along the dark road. The little animal drew his burden very slowly, the cart creaking and rocking noisily over the uneven road. Now and then Denis Donohoe spoke to him encouragingly, softly, his gaze at the same time going to the east, searching the blank sky for a hint of the dawn to come.

But they had gone rocking and swaying along the winding road for a long time before the day dawned. Denis Donohoe marked the spread of the light, the slow looming up of a range of hills, the sweep of brown patches of bog, then grey and green fields, broken by the glimmer of blue lakes, slopes of brown furze making for them a dull frame.

'Now that we have the blessed light we won't feel the journey at all,' Denis Donohoe said to the donkey. The ass drew the creel of turf more briskly, shook his winkers and swished his tail. When they struck very sharp hills Denis Donohoe got to the back of the cart, put his hands to the shafts, and, lowering his head, helped to push up the load, the muscles springing taut at the back of his thick limbs as he pressed hard against the bright frosty ground.

As they came down from the hills he already felt very hungry, his fingers tenderly fondling the slices of oaten bread he had put away in the pocket of his grey homespun coat. But he checked the impulse to eat, the long jaw of his swarthy face set, his strong teeth tight together awaiting the right hour to play their eager part. If he ate all the oaten bread now – splendid, dry, hard stuff, made of oat meal and water, baked on a gridiron – it would leave too long a fast afterwards. Denis Donohoe had been brought up to practise caution in these matters, to subject his stomach to a rigorous discipline, for life on the verge of a bog is an exacting business. Instead of obeying the impulse to eat Denis Donohoe blew warm breaths into his purple hands, beat his arms about his body to deaden the bitter cold, whistled, took some steps of an odd dance along the road, and went on talking to the donkey as if he were making pleasant conversation to a companion. The only sign of life to be seen on earth or air was a thin line of wild duck high up in the sky, one group making wide circles over a vivid mountain lake.

Half way on his journey to the country town Denis Donohoe pulled up his little establishment. It was outside a lonely cottage exactly like his own home. There was the same brown thatch on the roof, a garland of verdant wild creepers drooping from a spot at the gable, the same two small windows without any sashes in the front wall, the same narrow rutty pathway from the road, the same sort of yellow hen crackling heatedly, her legs quivering as she clutched the drab half door, the same scent of decayed cabbage leaves in the air. Denis Donohoe took a sack of hay from the top of the creel of turf, and spread some of it on the side of the road for the donkey. While he did so a woman who wore a white cap, a grey bodice, a thick woollen red petticoat, under which her bare lean legs showed, came to the door, waving the yellow hen off her perch.

'Good day to you, Mrs. Deely,' Denis Donohoe said, showing his strong teeth.

'Welcome, Denis, won't you step in and warm yourself at the fire, for the day is sharp, and you are early on the road?'

Denis Donohoe sat with the woman by the fire for some time, their exchange of family gossip quiet and agreeable. The young man was, however, uneasy, glancing about the house now and then like one who missed something. The woman, dropping her calm

33

eyes on him, divined his thoughts.

'Agnes is not about,' she said. 'She started off for the Cappa Post Office an hour gone, for we had tidings that a letter is there for us from Sydney.'

'A letter from her sister?'

'Yes, Mary is married there and doing well.'

Denis Donohoe resumed his journey.

At the appointed spot he ravenously devoured the oaten bread, then stretched himself on his stomach on the ground and took some draughts of water from a roadside stream, drawing it up with a slow sucking noise, his teeth chattering, his eyes on the bright pebbles that glittered between some green cress at the bottom. When he had finished the donkey also laved his thirst at the spot.

He reached the market town while it was yet morning. He led the creel of turf through the straggling streets, where some people with the sleep in their eyes were moving about. The only sound he made was a low word of encouragement to the donkey.

'How much for the creel?' a man asked, standing at his shop door.

'Six shilling,' Denis Donohoe replied, and waited, for it was above the business of a decent turf-seller to praise his wares or press for a sale.

'Good luck to you, son,' said the merchant, 'I hope you'll get it.' He smiled, folded his hands one over the other, and retired to his shop.

Denis Donohoe moved on, saying in an undertone to the donkey, 'Gee-up, Party. That old fellow is no good.'

There were other inquiries, but nobody purchased.

They said that money was very scarce. Denis Donohoe said nothing; money was too remote a thing for him to imagine how it could be ever anything else except scarce. He grew tired of going up and down past shops where there was no sign of business, so he drew the side streets and laneways, places where children screamed about the road, where there was a scent of soapy water, where women came to their doors and looked at him with eyes that expressed a slow resentment, their arms bare above the elbows, their hair hanging lankly about their ears, their voices, when they spoke, monotonous, and always sounding a note of tired complaint.

On the rise of a little bridge Denis Donohoe met a red-haired woman, a family of children skirmishing about her; there was a battle light in her wolfish eyes, her idle hands were folded over her stomach.

'How much, gossoon?' she asked.

'Six shillings.'

'Six devils!' She walked over to the creel, handling some of the sods of turf. Denis Donohoe knew she was searching a constitutionally abusive mind for some word contemptuous of his wares. She found it at last, for she smacked her lips. It was in the Gaelic. 'Spair-teach!' she cried -- a word that was eloquent of bad turf, dug from the first layer of the bog, a mere covering for the correct vein beneath it.

'It's good stone turf,' Denis Donohoe protested, a little nettled.

The woman was joined by some people who were hanging about, anxious to take part in bargaining which involved no personal liability. They argued, made jokes, shouted, and finally began to bully Denis Donohoe, the woman leading, her voice half a scream, her stomach heaving, her eyes dancing with excitement, a yellow froth gathering at the corners of her angry mouth, her hand gripping a sod of the turf, for the only dissipation life now offered her was this haggling with and shouting down of turf sellers. Denis Donohoe stood immovable beside his cart, patient as his donkey, his swarthy face stolid under the shadow of his broadbrimmed black hat, his intelligent eyes quietly measuring his noisy antagonists. When the woman's anger had quite spent itself the turf was purchased for five shillings.

Denis Donohoe carried the sods in his arms to the kitchen of the purchaser's house. It entailed a great many journeys in and out, the sods being piled up on his hooked left arm with a certain skill. His route lay through a small shop, down a semi-dark hallway, across a kitchen, the sods being stowed under a stairway where cockroaches scampered from the thudding of the falling sods.

Women were moving about the kitchen, talking incessantly, fumbling about tables, always appearing to search for something that had been lost, one crooning over a cradle that she rocked before the fire. The smell of cooking, the sound of something fatty hissing on a pan, brought a sense of faintness to Denis Donohoe, for he was ravenously hungry again.

He stumbled awkwardly in and out of the place with his armfuls of brown sods. The woman moved with reluctance out of his way. Once a servant girl raised the most melancholy pair of wide brown eyes he had ever seen, saying to him, 'It always goes through me to hear the turf falling in the stair-hole. It reminds me of the day I heard the clay falling on me father's coffin, God be with him and forgive him, for he died in the horrors.'

By the time Denis Donohoe had delivered the cartload of turf the little donkey had eaten all the hay in the sack. In the small shop Denis purchased some bacon, flour and tea, so that he had only some coppers to bring home with him. After some hesitation he handed back one penny for some biscuits, and these he ate as soon as he set out on the return journey.

The little donkey went over the road through the hills on the way back with spirit, for donkeys are good homers. Denis Donohoe sat up on the front of the cart, his legs dangling down beside the shaft. The donkey trotted down the slopes gayly, the harness rattling, the cart swaying, jolting, making an amazing noise.

The donkey cocked his ears, flecked his tail, even indulged in one or two buckjumps, as he rattled down the hilly roads. Denis Donohoe once or twice leaned out over the shaft, and brought his open hand down on the haunch of the donkey, but it was more a caress than a whack.

The light began to fade, the landscape to grow more obscure. Suddenly Denis Donohoe broke into song. They were going over a level stretch of ground. The donkey walked quietly. The quivering voice rang out over the darkening landscape gaining in quality and in steadiness, a clear light voice, the notes coming with the instinctive intonation, the perfect order of the born folk singer. It was some old Gaelic song, a refrain that had been preserved like the trunks of the primeval oaks in the bogs, such a refrain as might claim kinship with the Dresden Amen, sung by generations of German peasants until at last it reached the ears of Richard Wagner, giving birth to a classic. As he sang Denis Donohoe raised his swarthy face, his profile sharp against the pale sky, his eyes, half in rapture like all folk singers, ranging over the hills, his long throat palpitating, swelling, slackening like the throat of a bird quivering in song. Then a light from the sash-less windows of Mrs. Deely's cabin shone faintly and silence again brooded over the place. When he reached the cabin Denis Donohoe dismounted and walked into the kitchen, his eyes bright, his steps so eager that he became conscious of it and pulled up at once.

Mrs. Deely was sitting by the fire, her knitting needles busy. Denis Donohoe sat down beside her. While they were speaking a young girl came from the kitchen, stood beside the open fireplace.

'Agnes had great news from Australia from Mary,' Mrs. Deely said. 'She enclosed the price of the passage from this place to Sydney.'

'I'll be making the voyage the end of this month,' the girl herself added.

There was an awkward silence, during which Mrs. Deely carefully piloted one of her needles through an intricate turn in the heel of the sock.

'Well, I wish you luck, Agnes,' Denis Donohoe said at last, and then gave a queer odd little laugh, a little laugh that made Mrs. Deely regard him quickly and seriously. She noticed that he had his eyes fixed on the ground.

'It will be a great change from this place,' the girl said, fingering something on the mantelpiece. 'Mary says Sydney is a wonderful big city.'

Denis Donohoe slowly lifted his eyes, taking in the shape of the girl from the bare feet to the bright ribbon that was tied in her hair. What he saw was a slim girl, her limbs showing faintly in the folds of a cheap, thin skirt, a loose, small shawl resting on the shoulders, her bosom heaving gently where the shawl did not meet, her profile delicate and faint in the light of the fire, her eyes, suddenly turned upon him, being the eyes of a girl conscious of his eyes, her low breath the sweet breath of a girl stepping into her womanhood.

'Well, God prosper you, Agnes Deely,' Denis Donohoe said after some time, and rose from his seat.

The two women came out on the road to see him off. He did not dally, but jumped on to the front of the cart and rattled away.

Overhead the sky was winter clear, the stars merry, eternal, the whole heaven brilliant in its silent, stupendous song, its perpetual Magnificat; but Denis Donohoe made the rest of the journey in a black silence, gloom in the rigid figure, the stooping shoulders, the dangling legs; and the hills seemed to draw their grim shadows around his tragic ride to the lonely light in his mother's cabin on the verge of the dead brown bog.

2

There was a continuous clatter of conversation that rose and fell and broke like the waves on the beach;

there was the dull shuffling of uneasy feet on the ground, the tinkling of glasses, the rattle of bottles, and over it all the half hysterical laugh of a tipsy woman. Above the racket a penetrating, quivering voice was raised in song.

Now and again bleary eyes were raised to the stage, shadowy in a fog of tobacco smoke. The figure on the boards strutted about, made some fantastic steps, the face pallid in the streaky light, the mouth scarlet as a tulip for a moment as it opened wide, the muscles about the lips wiry and distinct from much practice, the words of the song coming in a vehement nasal falsetto and in a brogue acquired in the Bowery. The white face of the man who accompanied the singer on the piano was raised for a moment in a tired gesture that was also a protest; in the eyes of the singer as they met those of the accompanist was an expression of cynical Celtic humour; in the smouldering gaze of the pianist was the patient, stubborn sound of the Slav. The look between these entertainers, one from Connacht the other from Poland, was a little act of mutual commiseration and a mutual expression of contempt for the noisy descendants of the Lost Tribes who made merry in the place.

A Cockney who had exchanged Houndsditch for the Bowery leered up broadly at the Celt prancing about the stage. He turned to the companion who sat drinking with him, a tall, bony half-caste, her black eyes dancing in a head that quivered from an ague acquired in Illinois.

'E's all right, is Paddy,' said the voice from Houndsditch. He pointed a thumb that was a certifi-

40

cate of villainy in the direction of the stage.

'Sure,' said the coloured lady, whose ancestry rembled back away Alabama. She looked up at the stage with her bold eyes.

'I know him,' she said, thoughtfully. 'And I like him,' she added grinning. 'We all like him. He's one of the boys.' 'Wot price me?' said the Houndsditch man.

'Oh, you're good, too,' said the coloured lady. 'Blow in another cocktail, honey.' She struck her breast where the uneasy bone showed through the dusky skin. 'I've a fearful thirst right there.'

Little puckers gathered about the small, humorous eyes of the Cockney as he looked at her. 'My,' he said, 'you've got a thirst and a capacity, Old Sahara!'

The coloured lady raised the cocktail to her fat lips and as she did so there was a sudden racket, men shouting, women clapping their hands, the voice of the tipsy woman dominant in its hysteria over the uproar. The singer was bowing profuse acknowledgments from the stage, his eyes, sly in their cynical humour, upon the face of the Slav at the piano, his head thrown back, the pallor of his face ghastly.

The lady from Alabama joined in the tribute to the singer.

'Gore, 'core,' cried Old Sahara, raising her glass in the dim vapour. 'Here's to Denis Donohoe!'

III

The White Goat

1

The white goat stood in a little clearing closed in by a ring of whins on the hillside. Her head swayed from side to side like the slow motion of the pendulum of a great clock. The legs were a little spread, the knees bent, the sides slack, the snout grey and dry, the udder limp.

The Herd knew the white goat was in great agony. She had refused the share of bran he had brought her, had turned away from the armful of fresh ivy leaves his little daughter held out to her. He had desisted from the milking, she had moaned so continuously.

Some days before the Herd had found the animal injured on the hill; the previous night he had heard the labourers making a noise, shouting and singing, as they crossed from the tillage fields. He knew what had happened when he had seen the marks of their hob-nailed boots on her body. She was always a sensitive brute, of a breed that came from the lowlands. The sombre eyes of the Herd glowed in a smouldering passion as he stood helplessly by while the white goat swung her head from side to side.

He gathered some dry bracken and spread a bed of it near the white goat. It would be unkind to allow her to lie on the wet grass when the time came that she could no longer stand. He looked up at the sky and marked the direction of the wind. It had gone round to the west. Clouds were beginning to move across the sky. There was a vivid light behind the mountains. The air was still. It would rain in the night. He had thought for the white goat standing there in the darkness, sway-ing her head in agony, the bracken growing sodden at her feet, the rain beating into her eyes. It was a cold place and wind-swept. Whenever the white goat had broken her tether she had flown from it to the lowlands. He remembered how, while leading her across a field once, she had drawn back in some terror when they had come to a pool of water.

'The Herd looked at his little daughter. The child had drawn some distance away, the ivy leaves fallen from her bare arms. He was conscious that some fear had made her eyes round and bright. What was it that the child feared? He guessed, and marvelled that a child should understand the strange thing that was about to happen up there on the hill. The knowledge of Death was shining instinctively in the child's eyes. She was part of the stillness and greyness that was creeping over the hillside.

'We will take the white goat to the shelter of the stable,' the Herd said.

The child nodded, the fear still lingering in her eyes. He untied the tether and laid his hand on the horn of the goat. She answered to the touch, walking patiently but unsteadily beside him.

After a while the child followed, taking the other horn, gently, like her father, for she had all his under-standing of and nearness to the dumb animals of the fields. They came slowly and silently. The light failed rapidly as they came down the hill. Everything was merged in a shadowy vagueness, the colour of the white goat between the two dim figures alone proclaiming itself. A kid bleated somewhere in the distance. It was the cry of a young thing for its suckle, and the Herd saw that for a moment the white goat raised her head, the instinct of her nature moving her. Then she tottered down the hill in the darkness.

When they reached the front of the stable the white goat backed painfully from the place. The Herd was puzzled for a moment. Then he saw the little pool of water in a faint glimmer before their feet. He brought the animal to one side, avoiding it, and she followed the pressure of his directing hand.

He took down a lantern that swung from the rafters of the stable and lighted it. In a corner he made a bed of fresh straw. The animal leaned over a little against the wall, and they knew she was grateful for the shelter and the support. Then the head began to sway in a weary rhythm from side to side as if the pain drove it on. Her breath quickened, broke into little pants. He noted the thin vapour that steamed from about her body. The Herd laid his hand on her snout. It was dry and red hot. He turned away, leading the child by the hand, the lantern swinging from the other, throwing long yellow streaks of light about the gloom of the stable. He closed the door softly behind him.

It was late that night when the Herd got back from his rounds of the pastures. His boots soaked in the wet ground and the clothes clung to his limbs, for the rain had come down heavily. A rumble of thunder sounded over the hills as he raised the latch of his door. He felt glad he had not left the white goat tethered in the whins on the hill.

His little daughter had gone to sleep. His wife told him the child on being put to bed had wept bitterly, but refused to confess the cause of her grief. The Herd said nothing, but he knew the child had wept for the white goat. The thought of the child's emotion moved him, and he turned out of the house again, standing in the darkness and the rain. Why had they attacked the poor brute? He asked the question over and over again, but only the rain beat in his face and around him was darkness, mystery. Then he heard the voices higher up on the side of the hill, first for a laugh, then some shouts and cries. A thick voice raised the refrain of a song, and it came booming through the murky atmosphere. The Herd could hear the words:

> Where are the legs with which you run?
> Hurroo! Hurroo!
> Where are the legs with which you run
> When first you went to carry a gun?
> Indeed your dancing days are done!
> Och, Johnny, I hardly knew ye!

And then came the chorus like a roar down the hills:

> With drums and guns, and guns and drums
> The enemy nearly slew ye!

My darling dear, you look so queer,
Och, Johnny, I hardly knew ye!

The voices of the labourers passing from the tillage fields died away, and the rumble of thunder came down more frequently from the hills. The Herd crossed his garden, his boots sinking in the soft ground. Half way across he paused, for a loud cry had dominated the fury of the breaking storm. His ears were quick for the cries of animals in distress. He went on rapidly toward the stable.

The ground grew more sloppy and a thin stream of water came from the rim of his face. He noted the flashes of lightning overhead. Through it all the cry of the white goat sounded, with that weird, vibrating 'mag-gag' that was the traditional note of her race. It had a powerful appeal for the Herd. It stirred a feeling of passion within him as he hurried through the rain.

How they must have lacerated her, a poor brute chained to the sod, at the mercy of their abuse! The red row of marks along her gams, raw and terrible, sprang to his sight out of the darkness. Vengeance, vengeance! He gripped his powerful hands, opening and closing the fists. Then he was conscious of something in the storm and the darkness, that robbed him of his craving for personal vengeance. All that belonged to the primitive man welled up in him. He knew that in the heart of the future there lurked a reckoning – something, somebody – that would count the tally at the appointed time. Then he had turned round the gable of the stable. He saw the ghostly white thing, shadowy in the blackness, lying prostrate before the door. He stood still, his breath drawn inward.

There was a movement in the white shape. He could discern the blurred outline of the head of the animal as she raised it up a little. There was a low moan followed by a great cry. The Herd stood still, terror in his heart. For he interpreted that cry in all the terrible inarticulate consciousness of his own being. That cry sounded in his ears like an appeal to all the generations of wronged dumb things that had ever come under the lash of this tyranny of men. It was the protest of the brute creation against humanity, and to the Herd it was a judgment. Then his eyes caught a murky gleam beside the fallen white shape, and the physical sense of things jumped back to his mind.

He remembered that in wet weather a pool of water always gathered before the stable door. He remembered that there was a glimmer of it there when he had led the white goat into the stable. He remembered how she had shown fear of it.

He stooped down over the white goat where she lay. Thin wisps of her hair floated about looking like dim wraiths against the blackness of the pool. He caught a look of the brown eyes and was aware that the udder and teats bulged up from the water. He sank down beside her, the water making a splash as his knees dropped into the place. The animal raised her head a little and with pain, for the horns seemed to weigh like lead. But it was an acknowledgment that she was conscious of his presence; then the head fell back, a gurgle sounding over one of the ears.

The Herd knew what had happened, and it was all very tragical to his mind. His wife had come out to the stable for something, and had left the door open behind her. The white goat, goaded by the growing pain, had staggered out the door, perhaps feeling some desire for the open fields in her agony. Then she had seen before the threshold of the door that which had always been a horror to her – a pool of water. The Herd could see her tottering and swaying and then falling into it with a cry, fulfilling her destiny. He wondered if he himself had the same instinct for the things that would prove fatal to him? Why was he always so nervous when he stooped to or lay upon the ground? Why did it always give him a feeling that he would be trampled under the hooves of stampeding cattle rounded up for treatment for the warble fly? He trembled as he heard the beat of hooves on the ground behind him. He peered about and for a while did not recognise the shape that moved restlessly about in the darkness. He heard the neigh of the brood mare. He knew then she had been hovering about the stable afraid to go in out of the storm. She was afraid to go in because of the thing that lay before the stable door. He heard the answering call of the young foal in the stable, and he knew that it, too, was afraid to come out even at the call of its dam. Death was about in that night of storm, and all things seemed conscious of it.

He stooped down over the white goat and worked his hands under her shoulders. He lifted her up and felt the strain all over his frame, the muscles springing tense on his arms. She was a dead weight, and he had always prided on her size. His knees dug into the puddle in the bottom of the pool as he felt the pressure of his haunches. He strained hard as he got one of his feet under him. With a quick effort he got the other foot into position and rose slowly, lifting the white form out of the pool. The shaggy hair hung from the white goat, limp and reeking, numerous thin steams of water making a little ripple as they fell. The limbs of the Herd quivered under the weight, he staggered back, his heavy boots grinding in the gravel; then he set his teeth, the limbs steadied themselves, he swayed uncertainly for a moment, then staggered across the stable door, conscious of the hammer strokes of the heart of the white goat beating against his own heart. He laid her down in the bed of straw and heard the young foal bounding out of the stable in terror. The Herd stood in the place, the sweat breaking out on his forehead, then dropping in great beads.

The white goat began to moan. The Herd was aware from the rustling of the straw that her limbs were working convulsively. He knew from the nature of her wounds that her death would be prolonged, her agonies extreme. What if he put her out of pain? It would be all over in a moment. His hand went to his pocket, feeling it on the outside. He made out the shape of the knife, but hesitated.

One of the hooves of the white goat struck him on the ankle as her limbs worked convulsively. His hand went into his pocket and closed around the weapon. He would need to be quick and sure, to have a steady hand, to make a swift movement. He allowed himself some moments to decide. Then the blade of the knife shot back with a snap.

The sound seemed to reach the white goat in all its grim significance. She struggled to her feet, moaning more loudly. The Herd began to breathe hard. He was afraid she would cry out even as she had cried out as she lay in the pool before the stable door. The terror of the things that made up that cry broke in upon the Herd. He shook with fear of it. Then he stooped swiftly, his fingers nervously feeling over the delicate course of the throat of the white goat. His hands moved a little backwards and forwards in the darkness. He felt the hot stream on his hands, then the animal fell without a sound, her horns striking against the wall. He stood over for a moment and was conscious that his hands were wet. Then he remembered with a shudder that the whole tragedy of the night had been one of rains and pools and water and clinging damp things, of puddles and sweats and blood. Even now the knife he held in his fingers was dripping. He let it fall. It fell with a queer thud, sounding of flesh, of a dead body. It had fallen on the dead body of the white goat. He turned with a groan and made his way uncertainly for the stable door.

At the door he stood, thoughts crowding in upon, questions beating upon his brain and giving no time for answer. Around him was darkness, mystery, Death. What right had he to thrust his hand blindly into the heart of this mystery? Who had given him the power to hasten the end, to summon Death before its time? Had not Nature her own way for counting out the hours and the minutes? Had not she, or some other power, appointed an hour for the white goat to die? She would live, even in agony, until they could bear her up no longer; and having died Nature would pass her through whatever channel her laws had ordained. Had not the white goat made her last protest against his interference when she had risen to her feet in her death agony? And if the white goat, dumb beast that she was, had suffered wrong at the hands of man, then there was, the Herd now knew, a Power deliberate and inexorable, scrupulous in its delicate adjustment of right and wrong, that would balance the account at the appointed audit.

He had an inarticulate understanding of these things as he moved from the stable door. He tripped over a barrow unseen in the darkness and fell forward on his face into the field. As he lay there he heard the thudding of hooves on the ground. He rose dizzy and unnerved, to see the dim shapes of some cattle that had gathered down about the place from the upland. He felt the rain beating upon his face, the clothes hung dank and clammy to his limbs. His boots soaked and slopped when he stepped. A boom of thunder sounded overhead and a vivid flash of lightning lit up for an instant a great elm tree. He saw all its branches shining with water, drops glistening along a thousand stray twigs. Then the voices of the labourers returning over the hills broke in upon his ears. He heard their shouts, the snatches of their songs, their noise, all the ribaldry of men merry in their drink.

The Herd groped through the darkness for his house like a half-blind man, his arms out before him, and a sudden gust of wind that swept the hillside shrieked about the blood of the white goat that was still wet upon his hands.

IV

Michael and Mary

I

Mary had spent many days gathering wool from the whins on the headland. They were the bits of wool shed by the sheep before the shearing. When she had got a fleece that fitted the basket she took it down to the canal and washed it. When she had done washing it was a soft, white, silky fleece. She put it back in the brown sally basket, pressing it down with her long, delicate fingers. She had risen to go away, holding the basket against her waist, when her eyes followed the narrow neck of water that wound through the bog.

She could not follow the neck of yellow water very far. The light of day was failing. A haze hung over the great Bog of Allen that spread out level on all sides of her. The boat loomed out of the haze on the narrow neck of the canal water. It looked, at first, a long way off, and it seemed to come in a cloud. The soft rose light that mounted the sky caught the boat and burnished it like dull gold. It came leisurely, drawn by the one horse, looking like a Golden Barque in the twilight. Mary put her brown head a little to one side as she watched the easy motion of the boat. The horse drew himself along deliberately, the patient head going up and down with every heavy step. A crane rose from the bog, flapping two lazy wings across the wake of the boat, and, reaching its long neck before it, got lost in the haze.

The figure that swayed by the big arm of the tiller on The Golden Barque was vague and shapeless at first, but Mary felt her eyes following the slow movements of the body. Mary thought it was very beautiful to sway every now and then by the arm of the tiller, steering a Golden Barque through the twilight.

Then she realised suddenly that the boat was much nearer than she thought. She could see the figures of the men plainly, especially the slim figure by the tiller. She could trace the rope that slackened and stretched taut as it reached from the boat to the horse. Once it splashed the water, and there was a little sprout of silver. She noted the whip looped under the arm of the driver. Presently she could count every heavy step of the horse, and was struck by the great size of the shaggy fetlocks. But always her eyes went back to the figure by the tiller.

She moved back a little way to see The Golden Barque pass. It came from a strange, far-off world, and having traversed the bog went away into another unknown world. A red-faced man was sitting drowsily on the prow. Mary smiled and nodded to him, but he made no sign. He did not see her; perhaps he was asleep. The driver who walked beside the horse had his head stooped and his eyes on the ground. He did not look up as he passed. Mary saw his lips moving, and heard him mutter to himself; perhaps he was praying. He was a shrunken, misshaped little figure and kept step with the brute in the journey over the bog. But Mary felt the gaze of the man by the tiller upon her. She raised her eyes.

The light was uncertain and his peaked cap threw a shadow over his face. But the figure was lithe and youthful. He smiled as she looked up, for she caught a gleam of his teeth. Then the boat had passed. Mary did not smile in return. She had taken a step back and remained there quietly. Once he looked back and awkwardly touched his cap, but she made no sign.

When the boat had gone by some way she sat down on the bank, her basket of wool beside her, looking at The Golden Barque until it went into the gloom. She stayed there for some time, thinking long in the great silence of the bog. When at last she rose, the canal was clear and cold beneath her. She looked into it. A pale new moon was shining down in the water.

Mary often stood at the door of the cabin on the head land and watching the boats that crawled like black snails over the narrow streak of water through the bog. But they were not all like black snails now. There was a Golden Barque among them. Whenever she saw it she smiled, her eyes on the figure that stood by the shaft of the tiller.

One evening she was walking by the canal when The Golden Barque passed. The light was very clear and searching. It showed every plank, battered and tar-stained, on the rough hulk, but for all that it lost none of its magic for Mary. The little shrunken driver, head down, the lips moving, walked beside his horse. She heard his low mutters as he passed. The red-faced man was stooping over the side of the boat, swinging out a vessel tied to a rope, to haul up some water. He was singing a ballad in a monotonous voice. A tall, dark, spare man was standing by the funnel, looking vacantly ahead. Then Mary's eyes travelled to the tiller.

Mary stepped back with some embarrassment when she saw the face. She backed into a hawthorn that grew all alone on the canal bank. It was covered with bloom. A shower of the white petals fell about her when she stirred the branches. They clung about her hair like a wreath. He raised his cap and smiled. Mary did not know the face was so eager, so boyish. She smiled a little nervously at last. His face lit up, and he touched his cap again.

The red-faced man stood by the open hatchway going into the hold, the vessel of water in his hand. He looked at Mary and then at the figure beside the tiller.

'Eh, Michael?' the red-faced man said quizzically. The youth turned back to the boat, and Mary felt the blush spreading over her face.

'Michael!'

Mary repeated the name a little softly to herself. The gods had delivered up one of their great secrets.

She watched The Golden Barque until the two square slits in the stern that served as port holes looked like two little Japanese eyes. Then she heard a horn blowing. It was the horn they blew to apprise lock-keepers of the approach of a boat. But the nearest lock was a mile off. Besides, it was a long, low sound the horn made, not the short, sharp, commanding blast they blew for lock-keepers. Mary listened to the low sound of the horn, smiling to herself. Afterwards the horn always blew like that whenever The Golden Barque was passing the solitary hawthorn.

Mary thought it was very wonderful that The Golden Barque should be in the lock one day that she was travelling with her basket to the market in the distant village. She stood a little hesitantly by the lock. Michael looked at her, a welcome in his eyes.

'Going to Bohermeen?' the red-faced man asked.

'Ay, to Bohermeen,' Mary answered.

'We could take you to the next lock,' he said, 'it will shorten the journey. Step in.'

Mary hesitated, as he held out a big hand to help her to the boat. He saw the hesitation and turned to Michael.

'Now, Michael,' he said.

Michael came to the side of the boat, and held out his hand. Mary took it and stepped on board. The red-faced man laughed a little. She noticed that the dark man who stood by the crooked funnel never took his eyes from the stretch of water before him. The driver was already urging the horse to his start on the bank. The brute was gathering his strength for the pull, the muscles standing out on his haunches. They glided out of the lock.

It was half a mile from one lock to another. Michael had bidden her stand beside him at the tiller. Once she looked up at him and she thought the face shy but very eager, the most eager face that ever came across the bog from the great world.

Afterwards, whenever Mary had the time, she would make a cross-cut through the bog to the lock. She would step in make the mile journey with Michael on The Golden Barque. Once, when they were journeying together, Michael slipped something into her hand. It was a quaint trinket, and shone like gold.

'From a strange sailor I got it,' Michael said.

Another day that they were on the barque, the blinding sheets of rain that often swept over the bog came upon them. The red-faced man and the dark man went into the hold. Mary looked about her, laughing. But Michael held out his great waterproof for her. She slipped into it and he folded it about her. The rain pelted them, but they stood together, Michael holding the big coat folded about her. She laughed a little nervously.

'You will be wet,' she said.

Michael did not answer. She saw the eager face coming down close to hers. She leaned against him a little and felt the great strength of his arms about her. They went sailing away together in The Golden Barque through all the shining seas of the gods.

'Michael,' Mary said once, 'is it not lovely?'

'The wide ocean is lovely,' Michael said. 'I always think of the wide ocean going over the bog.'

'The wide ocean!' Mary said with awe. She had never seen the wide ocean. Then the rain passed. When the two men came up out of the hold Mary and Michael were standing together by the tiller.

Mary did not go down to the lock after that for some time. She was working in the reclaimed ground on the headland. Once the horn blew late in the night. It blew for a long time, very softly and lowly. Mary sat up in bed listening to it, her lips parted, the memory of Michael on The Golden Barque before her. She heard the sound dying away in the distance. Then she lay back on her pillow, saying she would go down to him when The Golden Barque was on the return journey.

The figure that stood by the tiller on the return was

not Michael's. When Mary came to the lock the red-faced man was telling out the rope, and where Michael always stood by the tiller there was the short figure of a man with a pinched, pock-marked face.

When the red-faced man wound the rope round the stump at the lock, bringing the boat to a stand-still, he turned to Mary.

'Michael is gone voyaging,' he said.

'Gone voyaging?' Mary repeated.

'Ay,' the man answered. 'He would be always talking to the foreign sailors in the dock where the canal ends. His eyes would be upon the big masts of the ships. I always said he would go.'

Mary stood there while The Golden Barque was in the lock. It looked like a toy ship packed in a wooden box.

'A three-master he went in,' the red-faced man said, as they made ready for the start. 'I saw her standing out for the sea last night, Michael is under the spread of big canvas. He had the blood in him for the wide ocean, the wild blood of the rover.' And the red-faced man, who was the Boss of the boat, let his eyes wander up the narrow neck of water before him.

Mary watched The Golden Barque, moving away, the grotesque figure standing by the tiller. She stayed there until a pale moon was shining below her, turning over a little trinket in her fingers. At last she dropped it into the water.

It made a little splash, and the vison of the crescent was broken.

V

The Haven

The long journey over the bog was tiring to the men.
They sat about, melancholy and silent, for the hours it
lasted. Hike trudged along in the path on the bank,
stumbling over the rough ground, muttering and praying as he went. Calcutta kept his sentry by the funnel.
The Boss hummed monotonously as he wandered about
the boat.

There was a little movement, signs of revived
interest in the world, as the brown bogland began to
merge in the green pastures. A man whistled when they
made the wooded places. The boat seemed to glide
faster under the great boughs of the overhanging trees.
The hoofs of the horse sounded sharp from the granite
road, houses sprang up on the landscape, men were to
be seen on the hillsides, carts rumbled along the roads.
There was a bend in the canal; the men strained their
eyes to round it, for round that bend was civilisation
and The Haven.

First, the eyes of the men caught the red tiles
crowning the roof; slowly the entire roof came to view,
then the yellow gable with the open window, the well-
known front, with its dark green paint edged with thin
gold lines, folded itself out, and the white lettering over
the door, 'The Haven', shone to the hungry eyes of the
crew. Even Hike, the driver, had been known to raise

his head at that bend of the canal.

The boat glided up to the limestone landing-place, and nowhere was she steered with a more delicate tiller. Calcutta stepped lightly ashore, a rope in his hand, wound it about the waiting stump, and the boat, straining hard, was brought to a stand-still. As he unwound the rope from the stump he wiped his dry mouth with his hand, and raised friendly eyes to The Haven. At the same moment the grotesque figure left the tiller, the Boss came from behind the funnel, both their feet touching the ground with military precision. Hike was leading the unyoked horse away to the stables below the village, the cross-bolt jolting on the great haunches of the brute. As the crew of three crossed the road to The Haven, the Boss hummed pleasantly, his eyes on Calcutta's fingers as they jingled some coppers.

Hanks of onions and some brushes made a drapery around the door, swaying in the breeze. When the men stepped into the shop it exhaled a scent of seeds. They were about in bags. The mouth of one sack was folded back. A farmer stood over it, turning a tuber in his hand, his mind given up to the good things of the season. A woman in a grey shawl was handling some pieces of bacon on the counter, her pale, cold eyes filled with that battle-light which shortens the lives of shop assistants in wayside places.

Crockery ware, tins of biscuits, white firkins of lard, yellow pyramids of cheeses rose out of the dimly-lighted spaces overhead. But the men from the boat passed through the oak-stained partition, with high lights of coloured glass. Behind this gilded place was the sanctuary they sought.

It was a long, narrow bar. The counter was high, and of oak. The display of galleries of bottles gave an air of opulence to the place that pleased the men. The girth of the golden-hooped barrels was reassuring. The men sat down on an aesthetic form, facing this display, their feet in sawdust, their hearts filled with the goodness of The Haven.

A dark-haired young man stood at professional attention behind the counter, his hand resting lightly on the cream-coloured handle of the patent cork-puller. Some little feathers clung to his hair. His eyes had a suggestion of bleariness. He left the impression of one who had risen early and hurriedly in some lofty attic. His complexion had moved down to the lower reaches of the jaws. It lingered there in a faded purple glory.

A spare, thin person, with drooping shoulders, was standing at the counter, looking vaguely into a pint measure half emptied. His thoughts were plainly regretful; he did not even look up when Calcutta orderd the first round. When the men got the measures in their hands they looked into them and forgot the long journey over the bog. The Boss stretched his legs out luxuriously before him, his heels tearing two little dark streaks in the sawdust on the floor.

The wall opposite the bar was taken up with stuff that seemed to flow over from the business outside. Great black pots were hanging from holdfasts. Coils of ropes, wire-netting, milk-strainers, tin cans, hay-rakes, reaping hooks, scythes, packages of sheep-dipping powder, reached up to the ceiling. They suggested husbandry, even industry. Opposite to them blazed the shelves of bottles, the barrels with the great golden hoops about their girths.

But the sense of these antagonisms was lost on the men. They had their backs steadily upon the symbols of industry. The second measure was already in their hands, their fingers about the glasses in a mild sort of ecstasy, devotional eyes upturned to the blazing shelves opposite, a holy silence upon them.

The oak-stained door of the partition swung open on its noiseless springs and a few men came in. They were from another boat that had just arrrived. The driver had the whip, which he never used, looped about his body. One of the group took a stride down the floor, his limbs well apart, rubbed his chin with his hand, gazed contemplatively upon the barman for a little and then ordered, as if in an afterthought, the most obvious of drinks.

One of these men wore an oil-coat of great capacity. The outlines of his figure were barge-like. His face peered out from under a pilot-hat with that intense gaze ahead acquired by those long afloat. The other men knew him to be one who had been at ferry work at the mouth of a river. Circumstances had compelled him to drift into the more secluded reaches of the canal. He was now in charge of a turfboat. The men admired the manner in which he disposed of his first drink.

'Now, men, time is passing. Come along,' he said, his oil-coat flapping about him as he swung out.

Nobody followed.

A door leading to an unexpected yard and many stores was pushed open, and a man with a sack tied apron-fashion about him came in. He was a carpenter.

He ordered some nails. While the assistant outside went to fetch them, the carpenter, in an expert double shuffle of the feet, moved down to the end of the bar where the light was most romantic. Simultaneously the barman found the same centre, had a glass filled; it hopped by his hand on to the counter, got caught on the same hop by the carpenter, and its contents had vanished down his ready throat before the boatmen had realised what had happened. The nails a moment later were handed in from outside, and the voice of the carpenter was heard in the yard calling out to his apprentice: 'Tommy, buck up; what's delaying you?' Then there was the sound of planks falling from a cart.

'Terrible treatment to give the blessed drink,' one of the boatmen said, resuming contemplation of his own measure.

A young lad danced in, with an Irish terrier at his heels, bringing with him a whiff of tar and guano. The men knew him to be a sort of god – the son of the owner of The Haven. He had been going about all day, listening to the forbidden talk of the workmen, rat hunting with the terrier, cutting notches with his penknife in unlawful places. He tilted the elbow of an arm that held a foaming measure, and disappeared under a flap in the counter.

The skipper with the pilot-hat returned with some lock-keepers. He accepted refreshment at their request. Then he said: 'Now, men, time is passing. Come along,' and went out again.

Nobody followed.

A young girl, leading a small child by the hand, passed through to some inward and private recess of

The Haven. The heads of all the men jerked up and
followed the female vision as it passed. Their eyes
remained upon the thick black hair, tied with a bright
ribbon as it fell down her back. As they gazed upon it
they knew that according to the calander and the custom of the country this hair should long ago have been
put up. They knew then that the vision was one who
wanted to remain suspended in her youth by the hair
of her head.

'The youngest sister of the proprietor,' one of the men
having local knowledge said. 'Brought in to mind the
children.'

The barman had looked after the vision with a
certain pensive ambition and a slight heightening of
the complexion on the lower reaches of the jaws. The
Boss of The Golden Barque wondered vaguely if the
raven-haired barman would succeed.

The man in the pilot-hat returned, beaming cheerfully around him. He had fetched some carters. One of
them sang out the inevitable order. The skipper of the
turf boat did what was expected of him. Then he went
through the partition as breezily as before, saying:
'Now, men, time is passing. Come along.'

Nobody followed.

The men sat in a long silence on the form. There was
a great peace in the place. A brass kettle sang softly
over a spirit-lamp. Some flies buzzed overhead. The
barman sat down and resumed his reading of a
romance entitled, 'Anastasia and the Duke'. The golden
silence was only broken now and again by the soft pal-
pitation of a throat down which a drink was passing.
Then a voice said: 'What did he say?'

'He said, "Time is passing." '

The silence was resumed. The kettle sang and the flies buzzed overhead. Then there was a grump at the end of the form. It was followed by another spell of silence, during which the breathing of the barman, as he stooped over his book, became quite audible, for the romance had reached the chapter in which Anastasia stood in deadly peril of the armours of the Duke.

'What did you say?' The question was droned out from the shadows. The man at the end of the form turned his head round slowly and said:

'I say, who cares a curse for time?' and bringing round his head he hitched his back well up against the wall.

The proprietor passed through The Haven. The barman plunged his hands into a basin of water, and made a great show of washing glasses, his mind brought back with violence from the great scene of Anastasia's temptation. The proprietor was natty, fingering his waxed moustache, his head slightly stooped, his appearance preoccupied.

'Good-day to the men,' he said, without looking up. A moment later his voice was heard in the yard, sharply calling out some orders.

After some time the silence was again broken.

'A great man,' one of the group said, taking a pull at his measure.

'A great man,' another agreed, after some reflection. Then, after a long pause:

'Aye, a great man!' and the vague person who had all this time, in marked isolation, been meditating over his glass, woke up, finished his potion, and went out, wiping his lips with the back of his hand.

At the partition he met the man with the pilot-hat, who was followed by an assortment of ex-boatmen and carters. He broke into a splendid smile as a carter gave the inevitable order.

'Now, men, time is passing,' he said, reaching out for the first filled measure. It vanished.

The partition door was opened timidly, and the haggard face of Hike peered in. Then he slunk down by the men to the extreme end of the counter. There he drank his measure with his back to the others. Calcutta followed his movements with a gleam in his eyes. The Boss frowned, then they all stood up as if in protest.

They spat on the sawdust and hitched their trousers about their loins with the air of men who were bracing themselves to once more face a difficult world. Then they passed through the partition.

The woman in the grey shawl was still leaning over the counter, but the bacon had been put aside, and now her thin hands were carefully feeling over some skeins of wool thread. The assistant was still waiting on her, a look of stupour on his exhausted face.

The men stepped out from The Haven, a faint odour of onions following them across the road. Skirting the road was the yellow water of the canal. Drawn up against the bank were some laden boats, looking picturesque in the clear light of the spring day.

When they got on board The Golden Barque, the Boss paced up and down the deck while the others lay about, smoking. Presently Hike came out of The Haven, and passed sullenly down the road. Suddenly the voice of Calcutta rang out, commanding, insolent.

'Hike!' he shouted.

At the word Hike stood, obedient as a soldier who had been called to attention. A hoarse laugh of derision greeted his action.

Then the Boss saw the grotesque figure of Hike swing about on the road. His face, malicious and repulsive, leered up at the boat from between the humps on his shoulders. The large eyes shone with a sinister light as they were raised to the figure of Calcutta. The lips of the long mouth parted, showing some immense yellow teeth. There was something demoniacal, hellishly ugly and wicked, in the expression of Hike. The Boss noticed that Calcutta sprang to his feet from the box on which he had been reclining.

Hike came over to the bank just below The Golden Barque, the leer sustained on his face.

'You thought you had her, didn't you?' he demanded of Calcutta. 'She was to stay with you for ever, wasn't she? You were such a beauty nobody was ever to come between you.' The voice of Hike was thick with an ugly emotion.

Calcutta measured the figure of the half dwarf, and spat down at him. 'Go away and scratch your humps, you spawn of a dromaderry,' he cried.

'You were so happy together, weren't you? – a pair of cooing doves?' Hike drawled, covering and uncovering his yellow teeth. 'She wouldn't look at anyone else at all; no man would do for her but yourself; she loved you, did Mollie the Mermaid.'

At the name, Calcutta leapt to the side of the boat, but the Boss confronted him there.

'Go to the cabin,' he commanded.

'Let me down to the cripple,' Calcutta shouted. 'I'll shake hands with him.'

But Hike had moved away, his bullet-shaped head quivering between his humped shoulders, his queer cackle of a laugh dying down the road to the village.

Calcutta, his body twitching, went down to the cabin and drank several mugs of water in rapid succession, then threw himself on his back on the bunk, his blazing eyes riveted on the beam a few paces above him, his lusty voice breaking out into a series of ribald songs, one following the other to the same out-of-tune air without any pause.

The Boss stood over the hatch for some time listening to the rumble that filled the cabin beneath, Calcutta's vocalism so violent that all words were quite incoherent. Slowly the voice got into a sort of chant, and the words became understandable. Calcutta, glaring at the beam above him, was roaring:

'Oh, oh, oh, I rowled me love in the new-mown hay
I rowled me love in the new-mown hay,
I rowled me love in the new-mown hay,
Oh, oh, oh, when the cocks they crew in the maurnin!'

The Boss wondered where Calcutta had got his songs; perhaps in the Black Hole. The Boss kicked the lid on to the opening into the cabin, and then resumed his own tramp about the deck of The Golden Barque, wondering, and wondering in vain, as the quiet night settled over the peaceful place, why two men should hate each other so bitterly. He was unable to decide whether it was very tragical or very comical that memory of a woman should keep evergreen their bitterness. One man, the Boss knew, held in his memory that which brought him visions of a white angel in shining joy and glory in heaven; the other man, whose voice now rumbled weirdly beneath, remembered so much of his passion that he exultingly figured her as burning in hell for all eternity.

The Boss gave it up.

'We must unload to-morrow,' he said, his eyes roving over the cargo.

The Man with the Gift

For twenty-five years the Boss had gone up and down the worn cabin steps without a worry. His fists had grown accustomed to the feel of ropes, to the rolling up and down of barrels, and the swinging of boxes, at the loading and discharging of The Golden Barque. The motion of his limbs had come to be part of the ritual of the deck. He exhaled an odour of tar. His feet had flattened, his hands had rounded, his neck had developed a curve, throwing his face forward. His eyes were palely yellow, like the water of the canal. His vision had become concentrated drilling through the landscape like canals. His temperament was placid. His emotions rose and fell as mechanically as if they were regulated by invisible locks. He was as tame as a duck. His name was Martin Coughlan, and he was known, by stray words that followed his speech like a memory to have come from the North.

That torch of democracy — organisation — one day reached the backwash of existence. It found by its strange devices, of all people, Martin Coughlan. Up to that he had no sense of responsibility for the wrongs of the world, no brooding of the spirit in the problems of his day. His interests began at one harbour and ended at another. The things that he saw from the deck made up his world. They were good, and he was satisfied. But then they came to him and told him he had been elected on the Committee. He beamed at the announcement, for he grasped, though vaguely, that he was a man chosen, one to whom honour was paying her respects. He walked into the shed where they held the Committee meetings with his slow lurch, his mind a blank as to the purpose of the assembly. He made no inquiries. He sat down with the others and looked around him. A man at a table read something out of a book. Martin Coughlan laughed, and felt the other staring at him.

A deep voice, with a note of admonition, if not tragedy, called out 'Order'. Martin Coughlan poked the ribs of a neighbour to show that he appreciated the humour of the situation.

Then a man rose at the head of the table. He was a spare man with drooping moustachios, a penetrating eye, a voice that sounded high and sharp in the shed. Martin Coughlan stared at the speaker. Something rare and unsuspected had touched his life. He wondered where this spare man had got all the words. They came out in a steady flow. He was obviously aiming at something, but what it was Martin Coughlan did not know and, indeed, did not care. It was sufficient for him that the words came on and on. He had never heard any mortal before keeping up such a sustained flood of speech. Martin Coughlan leaned back, delight on his face.

Another man rose. He spoke even better. He gesticulated with energy. The others began to slap their limbs with their hands. Martin Coughlan slapped his limbs, feeling he was privileged. He had begun to live. A thick-set man followed. His voice wakened echoes all over the place. His eyes flashed around, seeking one face now, another again. Suddenly the eyes fell on Martin Coughlan; the man addressed him as if he were appealing to an intelligence. He argued with him, made gestures at him, deposited all his logic at his feet.

Martin Coughlan's blood began to heat. He felt a tingle of the curve on the back of his neck. He coughed to relieve the tension. Then the speaker's gaze wandered to somebody else.

The talk went on for some hours. Men grew excited. Several spoke at the same time for pregnant minutes. Martin Coughlan began to perspire. Once he shouted, 'Hear, hear' because the words had begun to sound familiar.

When the Committee meeting broke up he went back to the boat, his cheeks flaming, feeling that he had done it all himself. He passed Hike on the way. The little driver looked up at him with respect. The dark-faced man was sitting on a box by the stern.

'The meeting over?' he asked.

'Yes,' Martin Coughlan said.

His voice sounded hoarse. His throat felt dry. He went down to the keg and drank a mug of water.

Afterwards Martin Coughlan paced the deck with a new air. He became preoccupied. Once they saw him gesticulating at a bush on the bank. He took a new tone to the lock-keepers. He was always clearing his throat.

A few times at the meals they thought he was about to make a speech. But something always overcame him. When they sounded him as to the Committee proceedings his face beamed.

'There was speech-making,' he would say.

'What did they say?'

Martin Coughlan rose. He caught the lapel of his coat; struck an attitude. An inspired look came into his face. But no words followed. Instead he took up a bucket and went on deck.

'He's a great man for the Committee,' they said. 'He won't give the show away.'

'Aye, man, but that fellow is knowing. He could hold a Cabinet secret.'

One day the dark-faced man loaned a paper at a village.

'They don't give the speeches,' he said, 'but there is the name right enough – Martin Coughlan.'

Martin Coughlan took the paper. His eyes swam as he spelled out his name. He pored over the sheet for long spells throughout the rest of the evening. When the men were turning in he said: 'Boys, but she's a brave wee paper.'

He got a candle, and sat over it, spelling everything out, including the advertisements. Then he sat up, delight on his face, the look in his eyes of a man who knew he had achieved something. 'Men,' he said, 'I've overhauled her, beam and aft, stem to stern.'

But the only answer was a chorus of heavy snores. He turned in with a grumble.

There was another Committee meeting soon after. The speeches fell on his head like dew from the heavens. Language! Why, the world had never yet heard the like. Moreover, he became conscious that the other men were deferring to him in their views. He sat there as solemn as a judge, the greatest listener who had ever arrived in the shed. The speakers felt that they had at last got hold of an audience, a man of appreciation. Now and then he nodded his head in approval. It was worth a yard of debate. When he shook his head in disapproval it excited the speakers. They went on and on, fighting, arguing, playing for his opinion. But Martin Coughlan held to his silent views with wonderful pugnacity. He was not to be cajoled.

'What were they at last night, Martin?' one of the men asked afterwards.

'That,' said Martin, after a pause, 'is a secret.'

'He's too close-minded,' they said. 'He keeps it all in for the Committee. It must be something to hear him when the cork is off.'

The dark-faced man was fond of the paper. He got it regularly in the village. 'Here we are,' he said, with satisfaction. 'They give us the speeches this time. Now we'll know what Martin Coughlan had to say for himself.'

But there was no speech from Martin Coughlan. Everybody had said something except the representative from The Golden Barque.

The dark-faced man made a complaint.

'Don't mind the paper,' Martin Coughlan said. 'She is no good. I knew from the first she had sprung a leak.'

But he felt that the men were dissatisfied. He struck an attitude on the deck, and said: 'Mr. Chairman and gentlemen, – I venture to think.' he paused. 'To my mind,' he added. There was another pause. 'I say standing here to-night.' He looked vaguely over the landscape. 'I beg to propose.' And then he took a little run up and down the deck, rubbing his hands with delight.

'He's too clever,' one of the men said. 'He thinks to put us off by play-acting. It won't do.'

Before the proceedings of the next Committee meeting began, Martin Coughlan took the secretary aside. The secretary was a shrewd person. There was a motion on the agenda to give him a salary.

'John,' said Martin Coughlan, with familiarity. 'I want you to tell me how it is done.'

'How is what done?'

'The speeches, you know; the language, the words, the talk they do have.'

John was puzzled. Then a light broke upon him.

'Well,' he said, 'a man must have it in him.'

'Have what in him?'

John hesitated, thought, and said. 'The gift.'

Martin Coughlan was crestfallen. He felt there was something in life he had let slip.

'Where would there be likelihood of getting the gift?' he asked at last.

'I don't know,' the other replied. 'It comes from within.'

'Oh, I see,' Martin Coughlan said, more cheerfully. Then he confided, 'John I have it within in the inside of me. Language, great language. But I can't get it out.'

'Have courage,' the other said. 'Take your chance. Get up on your legs. Face them. When you do that the words will flow out of you.'

'Do you think they will, John?'

'Sure.' John was a man persuasive, one who carried conviction, inspired hope — and drew salaries.

'Then there is that wee paper, John. If I'd come out with the words they would be there, of course. They do be reading her, looking out for what a man might say.'

'Oh, that's it, is it, Martin?' John asked, then patted the other on the back. 'That will be all right, old man. Leave that to me. Vote straight on the salary question, and the goods will be delivered to you on the paper.

'Thanks, John. I will.'

At a critical moment in the debate, Martin Coughlan rose. He went over to the table, rapped his knuckles upon it to command attention, jerked the collar of his coat about his neck. He struck the attitude he had rehearsed aboard. It was reminiscent of various statues erected to the memory of great orators.

He looked up and down the shed. A hush fell upon the assembly. Men leaned back to hear what the silent man, the audience, the one man of reticence among them, had to say at this crisis.

'Mr. Chairman and Mr. Gentlemen,' Martin Coughlan began, blundering through nervousness.

There was a laugh. Martin Coughlan moistened his lips with his tongue, for they were dry and inclined to stick. One of his knees struck against the other. Then he had to clear a lump from his throat.

'John, our secretary,' he said at last, 'told me that if I stood up on me legs the words would flow out from within the inside of me.'

He hesitated, looking about him in a panic, a queer feeling of collapse in his brain. He smiled a ghastly smile.

'Go on,' said the chairman.

'He said,' Martin Coughlan resumed, his voice falling to an echo, 'that if I faced you they would flow out of me. But – by heavens – they won't.' He sat down. There was a burst of laughter and applause.

The men stared at Martin Coughlan. There was that mixture of scepticism, enjoyment, malicious delight, in their glances that fasten upon all fallen gods. They were taking their fun out of an exposure, the showing up of an emptiness that wore a mask, the betrayal of that discretion which is only a dullness.

Martin Coughlan was too heated, too full of confusion to notice their crude levity. By the time he had recovered himself they had dropped him. They no longer deferred to him. He was no longer appealed to as an intelligence. He drew back instinctively to the shadows, and he sat there until the meeting broke up.

When he reached his boat the men greeted him with deference. He muttered something and went down to the cabin. He stayed there for the rest of the night.

'The Committee,' he said to the dark-faced man next day, 'is a rotten Committee.'

'I thought that all along,' the other replied. 'But I didn't like to say it, seeing you were a great one on it.'

'And an ignorant Committee,' Martin Coughlan added.

'It is that.'

But by the end of the week the paper was out. The dark-faced man after reading it, looked up at Martin Coughlan and then went up to him.

'Look here, Boss,' he said, putting out his hand, 'shake hands.'

They shook hands, Martin Coughlan nervously.

'It was a great speech,' the dark-faced man said. 'You're wasting your time on this boat.'

Martin Coughlan blushed; his gaze was uncertain.

The other left him the paper.

He sat on a barrel and opened the sheet. There was his name in print again; he spelled it out slowly. 'Mr. Martin Coughlan, who was received with loud applause, said – ,' and there followed over a column of type, of words, of language, of a speech. He read it over with a thumping heart. It was dotted with 'hear, hear', 'applause', and 'cheers'. When he finished he stood up and walked the deck, his thick limbs outspread, his flat feet solid on the planks, his chest out.

'Is it a good report, Boss?' they asked.

'It is very fair, very fair, men,' he said, with toleration.

'Man, but I'd like to hear it coming out.'

'No doubt you would.'

'We'll hear you some time.'

'You will, why not, to be sure.' He ran his fingers through his hair. He drilled spaces, vague spaces, through the familiar landscape with his gaze. His blood rose gradually, eventually flooding his face until it grew purple in colour, rising as steadily as if somebody had lifted the sluice of a flood-gate.

'God, the language of it,' he repeated to himself over again throughout the day.

For the first time in his life, he refused to go into The Haven when they had made the journey across the bog. Instead he went into the cabin, and alone spelt the speech over and over again.

Gradually his mind got over the habit of thinking of it as something apart, something outside his own life. He no longer said, 'God, the language of it'. Instead he muttered, 'Great language; splendid talk; just the thing. That's it. That's what I'd say. That's the very word I'd say. I declare I think it was the word I said. It was going through my head at the time. I must have said that very word. If I did not, I intended it. But I forget what I said. Maybe I said it. To be sure I said it. Of course I said it. Why not? The very word; no, but the very words. If I said one word I must have said another. I could not help following up one word with another. What was to stop me? Nothing, I went on that very way. One word borrowed another. What else could it do. To be sure I said it. In fact, it's what I said, word for word.'

He went on persuading himself until the others came back from The Haven.

He went up to the dark-faced man.

'I tell you what it is, it's a very fine report; a very good report; a tip-top report. Word for word there it is, in black and in white.' He struck one fist in the other.

'Boss,' the other said, something almost approaching reverence in his long, narrow face, 'you're a great one, a gifted one. For to turn round and say the like of what you said, a man must have the gift.'

'To be sure he must,' Martin Coughlan agreed taking some steps along by the cargo covered with great oil-cloths. 'I told John, the secretary, I had it within in the inside of me. And what had I within in the inside of me, I ask you, men? The gift!'

'Well, thank God we'll all hear you soon,' the dark-faced man said. 'There's a public meeting coming on.'

Martin Coughlan drew a long breath. 'You don't tell me so?'

'I do. We had word of it in The Haven. There is to be

speech-making, and great speech-making. We'll expect you that day to show the great gift that's in you.'

'You will, to be sure,' Martin Coughlan said, but without enthusiasm. He ran his fingers through his hair. Then he walked away from the others, standing at the prow of the boat, his sturdy figure solid against the water.

'A great one he is for the gab,' the grotesque-looking man said irreverently. 'Look at the two powerful limbs he has holding him up from the ground.'

After that Martin Coughlan grew very subdued, silent, avoiding the topic of the coming meeting. The men said he was bottling himself up for the big occasion. They noted that he still pored over the paper that contained his speech. He would lie back in his bunk at night, a candle fixed by his side, drilling through the speech. Once or twice the men heard him muttering to himself like a boy grappling with a lesson. In these days it was noted that some of the colour left his face. A certain pensiveness crept into his expression.

'Boss,' one of the men asked him. 'Are you in pain?'

'I am,' Martin Coughlan answered, and walked sadly away.

Once the men wakened to hear him pacing the deck in the middle of the night. The dark-faced man went up the ladder and popped his vignette over the hold. He came back after a time.

'He's on deck in his shirt,' he said. 'The moon is shining on him, his legs are like two white pillars under the tiller. He has that paper with him. I heard him giving out a few words. He was losing them, trying to catch them up again, stumbling and staggering over them like a man that would be raving. Then he would run his hands through his hair, and the wind blowing the shirt about the white pillars.'

'Be the powers,' said the grotesque man, turning over in his bunk, 'it's a chilly sort of a night, and I'm glad I have not the gift.'

As the day of the meeting approached, and it became more and more a topic of conversation, Martin Coughlan's depression increased. Something seemed to weigh him down. He took the dark-faced man aside.

'You know this meeting is got up by the Committee?' he said.

'I do.'

'And you can call to mind what I told you of that Committee a long while ago. I said it was a rotten Committee.'

'You did. I remember that.'

'And I said it was an ignorant Committee.'

'You did, right enough.'

'You agreed with me. We were at one as regards this Committee. Very well, I'm not going to give that Committee the satisfaction of making a speech for them.'

'Now, that would be a pity and you having the gift.'

'There you are. That's what makes me do it. How can a man of gift speak for a rotten, ignorant Committee?'

To the dark-faced man this was a poser. Perhaps in that moment of expediency, of pressure, Martin Coughlan showed that he had, after all, some talent for politics.

He walked down the deck with a stride. 'Never!' he

exclaimed with decision, waving his arms.

The meeting came off without Martin Coughlan. He did not even attend. He 'sent word' to strike his name off the Committee.

'We will, indeed,' one of the men said. 'Little good any such tame duck is to anyone.'

The men from The Golden Barque were disappointed that Martin Coughlan did not pour forth his eloquence at the assembly. They somehow regarded him as in some way wronged. But he became more cheerful himself. He began to whistle again as he moved around the boat. His flat feet became more than ever a part of the ritual of the deck. The curve at the back of his neck threw out his head another degree. His eyes became more palely yellow. They went on digging imaginary canals in the landscape. He was happy as a duck in the water. Once the dark-faced man asked: 'Boss, what became of the paper with your speech in it?'

'Oh, you rag!' Martin Coughlan made answer, 'I rolled her up in a stone, and she's at the bottom a wheen of weeks.'

A Wayside Burial

The parish priest was in a very great hurry and yet anxious for a talk on his pet subject. He wanted to speak about the new temperance hall. Would I mind walking a little way with him while he did so? He had a great many things to attend to that day... We made our way along the street together, left the town behind us, and presently reached that sinister appendage of all Irish country towns, the workhouse. The priest turned in the wide gate, and the porter, old, official, spectacled, came to meet him.

'Has the funeral gone?' asked the priest, a little breathless.

'I'll see, Father.' The porter shuffled over de flags, a great door swung open; there was a vista of white-washed walls, a chilly vacant corridor, and beyond it a hall where old men were seated on forms at a long, white deal table. They were eating – a silent, grey, bent, beaten group. Through a glass partition we could see the porter in his office turning over the leaves of a great register.

'I find,' he said, coming out again, speaking as if he were giving evidence at a sworn inquiry, 'that the remains of Martin Quirke, deceased, were removed at 4.15.'

'I am more than half an hour late,' said the priest, regarding his watch with some irritation.

We hurried out and along the road to the country, the

priest trailing his umbrella behind him, speaking of the temperance hall but preoccupied about the funeral he had missed, my eyes marking the flight of flocks of starlings making westward.

Less than a mile of ground brought us to the spot where the paupers were buried. It lay behind a high wall, a narrow strip of ground, cut off from a great lord's demesne by a wood. The scent of decay was heavy in the place: it felt as if the spring and the summer had dragged their steps here, to lie down and die with the paupers. The uncut grass lay rank and grey and long – Nature's unkempt beard – on the earth. The great bare chestnuts and oaks threw narrow shadows over the irregular mounds of earth. Small, rude wooden crosses stood at the heads of some of the mounds, lopsided, drunken, weatherbeaten. No names were inscribed upon them. All the bones laid down here were anonymous. A robin was singing at the edge of the wood: overhead the rapid wings of wild pigeons beat the air.

A stable bell rang impetuously in the distance, dis-missing the workmen on the lord's demesne. By a freshly-made grave two gravediggers were leaning on their spades. They were paupers, too: men who got some privilege for their efforts in this dark strip of earth between the wood and the wall. One of them yawned. A third man stood aloof, a minor official from the workhouse: he took a pipe from his mouth as the priest approached.

The three men gave one the feeling that they were rather tired of waiting, impatient, to have their little business through. It was a weird spot in the gathering gloom of a November evening. The only bright thing in the place the only gay spot, the only cheerful patch of colour, almost exulting in its grim surroundings, was the heap of freshly thrown up soil from the grave. It was rich in colour as newly-coined gold.

Resting upon it was a clean, white, unpainted coffin. The only ornament was a tin breastplate on the lid and the inscription in black letters.

Martin Quirke
Died November 3, 1900
R.I.P.

The white coffin on the pile of golden earth was like the altar of some pagan god. I stood apart as the priest, vesting himself in a black stole, approached the grave-side and began the recital of the burial service in Latin. The gravediggers, whose own bones would one day be interred anonymously in the same ground, stood on either side of him with their spades, two grim acolytes. The minor official from the workhouse, the symbol of the State, bared a long narrow head, as white and as smooth as the coffin on the heap of earth. I stood by a groggy wooden cross, the eternal observer.

The priest spoke in a low monotone, holding the book close to his eyes in the uncertain light. And as he read I fell to wondering who our brother in the white coffin might be.

Some merry tramp who knew the pain and the joy of the road? Some detached soul who had shaken off the burden of life's conventions, one who loved lightly and took punishment casually? One who saw crime as a science or merely a broken reed? Or a soldier who had carried a knapsack in foreign campaigns? A creature of empire who had found himself in Africa, or Egypt, or India, or the Crimea, and come back again to claim his pile of golden earth in the corner of the lord's demesne? If the men had time, perhaps they would stick a little wooden cross over the spot where his bones were laid down... The priest's voice continued the recitation of the burial service and the robin sang at the edge of the dim wood. Down the narrow strip of rank burial ground a low wind cried, and the light, losing its glow in the western sky, threw a grey pall on the grass. And under the influence of the moment a little memory of people I had known and forgotten went across my mind, a memory of people who had at last got their white, clean coffin and their rest on a pile of golden earth, people who had gone like our brother in the dead boards... There was the man, the scholar, who had taught his school who had an intelligence, who could talk, who, perhaps, could have written only –. The wind sobbed down the narrow strip of ground... He had made his battle, only given way step by step, gradually but inexorably yielding ground to the thing that was hunting him out of civilised life. He had gone from his school, his home, his friends, fleeing from one miserable refuge to another in the miserable country town. Eventually he had passed in through the gates of the workhouse. It was all very vivid now – his attempts to get back to the life he had known, like a man struggling in the quicksands. There were the little spurts back to the town, the well-shaped head, the face which still held some remembrance of its distinction and its manhood erect over the quaking, broken frame;

that splendid head like a noble piece of sculpture on the summit of a crumbling ruin. Forth he would come, the flicker of resistance, a pallid battle-light in the eyes, a vessel that had been all but wrecked once more standing up the harbour to meet the winds that had driven it from the seas – and afar a little battle once more taking in the sheets and crawling back to the anchorage of the dark workhouse, there to suffer in the old way, in secret to curse, to pray, to despair, to hope, to contrive some little repairs to the broken physique in order that there might be yet another journey into waters that were getting more and more shadowy. And the day came when the only journey that could be made was a shuffle to the gate, the haunted eyes staring into a world which was a nightmare of regrets. How terrible was the pathos of that life, that struggle, that tragedy, how poignant its memory while the robin sang at the edge of the dim wood'... And there was that red-haired, defiant young man with the build of an athlete, the eyes of an animal. How bravely he could sing up the same road to the dark house'. It was to him as the burrow is to the rabbit. He would come out to nibble at the regular and lawful intervals, and having nibbled return to sleep and shout and fight for his 'rights' in the dark house. And once, on a spring day, he had come out with a companion, a pale woman in a thin shawl and a drab skirt, and they had taken to the roads together, himself swinging his ashplant, his stride and manner carrying the illusion of purpose, his eyes on everything and his mind nowhere; herself trotting over the broken shoes beside him, a pale shadow under the fire of his red head. They had gone away into a road whose milestones were dark houses, himself singing the song of his own life, a song of mumbled words, without air or music; herself silent, clutching her thin shawl over her breast, her feet pattering over the little stones of the road... The wind whistled down over the graves, by the wooden crosses... There was that little woman who at the close of the day, when the light was charitable in its obscurity, opened her door and came down from the threshold of her house, painfully as if she were descending from a great height. Nobody was about. All was quietness in the quiet street. And she drew the door to, put the key in the lock, her hand trembled, the lock clicked'. The deed was done'. Who but herself could know that the click of the key in the lock was the end, the close, the dreadful culmination of the best part of a whole century of struggle, of life? Behind that door she had swept up a bundle of memories that were now all an agony because the key had clicked in the lock. Behind the door was the story of her life and the lives of her children and her children's children. Where was the use, she might have asked, of blaming any of them now? What was it that they had all gone, all scattered, leaving her broken there of the last? Had not the key clicked in the lock? In that click was the end of it all; in the empty house were the ghosts of her girlhood, her womanhood, her motherhood, her old age, her struggles, her successes, her skill in running her little shop her courage in riding one family squall after another'. The key had clicked in the lock. She moved down the quiet street, sensitive lest the eye of the neighbours should see her, a tottering, broken thing going by the vague walls, keeping to the back streets, setting out for the dark house beyond the town. She had said to them, 'I will be no trouble to you.' And, indeed, she was not. They had little more to do for her than join her hands over her breast... The wind was plaintive in the gaunt trees of the dark wood... Which of us could say he would never turn a key in the lock of an empty house? How many casual little twists of the wrist of Fate stand between the best of us and the step down from the threshold of a broken home? What rags of memories have any of us to bundle behind the door of the empty house when the hour comes for us to click the key in the lock?... The wind cried down the narrow strip of ground where the smell of decay was in the grass.

There was a movement beside the white coffin, the men were lifting it off the golden pile of earth and lowering it into the dark pit.

The men's feet slipped and shuffled for a foothold in the yielding clay. At last a low, dull thud sounded up from the mouth of the pit. Our brother in the white coffin had at last found a lasting tenure in the soil. The official from the dark house moved over to me. He spoke in whispers, holding the hat an official inch of respect for dead above the narrow white shred of his skull.

'Martin Quirke they are burying,' he said.

'Who was he?'

'Didn't you ever hear tell of Martin Quirke?'

'No never.'

'A big man he was one time, with his acres around him and his splendid place. Very proud people they were – he and his brother – and very hot, too. The Quirkes of Ballinadee.'

'And now –.'

I did not finish the sentence. The priest was spraying the coffin in the grave with the golden earth.

'Ashes to ashes and dust to dust.' It fell briskly on the shallow deal timber.

'Twas the land agitation, the fight for the land, that brought Martin Quirke down,' said the official as the earth sprayed the pauper's coffin. 'He was one of the first to go out under the Plan of Campaign – the time of the evictions.

They never got back their place. When the settlement came the Quirkes were broken. Martin lost his spirit and his heart. Drink it was that got him in the end, and now –.'

'Requiem aeternam dona eis, Domine et lux perpetua luceat eis,' the priest's voice said.

'All the same,' said the official, 'it was men like Martin Quirke who broke the back of landlordism. He was strong and he was weak. God rest him.'

I walked away over the uneven ground, the memory of the land agitation, its bitterness and its passion, oppressing me. Stories of things such as this stalked the country like ghosts.

The priest overtook me, and we turned to leave. Down the narrow strip of the lord's demesne were the little pauper mounds, like narrow boxes wrapped in the long grey grass. Their pathos was almost vibrant in the dim November light. And away beyond them were a series of great heaps, looking like broad billows out to sea. The priest stood for a moment.

'You see the great mounds at the end?' he asked. 'They are the Famine Pits.'

'The Famine Pits.'

'Yes; the place where the people were buried in heaps and hundreds, in thousands, during the Famine of '46 and '47. They died like flies by the roadside. You see such places in almost every part of Ireland. I hope the people will never again die like that – die gnawing the gravel on the roadside.'

The rusty iron gate in the demesne wall swung open and we passed out.

SHORT STORIES OF PADRAIC PEARSE
Desmond Maguire
A dual language book

These five stories show us that Pearse was a man of deep understanding. He analyses the sorrows and joys of the Irish people of his time, and writes of the tragedies of life and death from which they could never escape.

THE STORMY HILLS
Daniel Corkery

Daniel Corkery, one of the most notable influences on Irish fiction, shared the faith and sensitivity of his people.

These are stories of great force and atmosphere. They tell of a life in a mountainy landscape and of man's struggle with the land. They are stories of people caught in the net of hardship and passion—with the pounding of the sea, the lovely hills and fields abandoned to nature.

ISLANDERS
Peadar O'Donnell

First published in 1927, this powerful novel depicts life in the early days of the twentieth century of a small island community off the Donegal coast. This is a story of epic simplicity, of people who confront in their daily lives, hunger, poverty and death by drowning.

WILDGOOSE LODGE AND OTHER STORIES

Volume One

In this, the first of an eight volume series of William Carleton's *Traits and Stories* we are given four works which display his genius in all its versatility and variety. 'The Lough Derg Pilgrim' is the earliest of his published pieces, and in this autobiographical tale he recalls his adventures at Lough Derg when, as a future candidate for holy orders, he first made that famous pilgrimage. The picaresque nature of the story and the wry, self-mocking quality of his reminiscence leavens the harrowing nature of the experience he recalls.

'Ned McKeown', the one totally comic tale of the four, immortalises in seemingly artless dialogue between the erring husband and his afflicted wife, the travails of Irish marriages and the consolations offered by the visitations of mysterious strangers to the hearth.

In 'The Lianhan Shee' and 'Wildgoose Lodge' the tone becomes progressively darker, shading perceptibly from ironic observation to tragic participation. In the first of these Carleton holds a mirror up to the Irish nature, reflecting in this tale the deeply superstitious Mary O'Sullivan and her confrontation with the tormented figure alienated from church and community, the Lianhan Shee. In 'Wildgoose Lodge' Carleton gives an intensely moving account of another aspect of Irish life and tells a nightmare tale, very much in the manner of Poe. Moving relentlessly from foreboding to tragic reality he recounts one of the darker episodes of Ribbonism.

DENIS O'SHAUGHNESSY   GOING
TO MAYNOOTH

Volume Two

'Denis O'Shaughnessy   going to Maynooth' is one of the most important nineteenth-century short stories. It is a novel re-creation of a perennial theme dear to the romantic throughout Europe, the hero in conflict with his environment. But Denis O'Shaughnessy is no Manfred or Childe Harold but a comic hero who may be at the mercy of his circumstances in every way except one—he can observe his own situation with a sense of comedy and an irony that he does not hesitate to turn on himself on occasions. This clarity of vision makes the story both a brilliant anti-autobiography and a gripping social document. It looks back to the Bildunsroman tradition of the Romantic movement started by Goethe in *Poetry and Truth* and forward to Joyce and Moore, as Professor Harmon shows in his introduction. Carleton's style may often be criticised for its lack of control over the material but in these two stories it is clearly vindicated. 'Neal Malone' is an extraordinary blend of fairy-story, folk-tale, social commentary and pure comedy. It can only be compared to one of Chaucer's *Canterbury Tales*, a fair tribute to the range and versatility of Carleton's style.

PHELIM O'TOOLE'S COURTSHIP
AND OTHER STORIES

Volume Three

In 'Phelim O'Toole's Courtship' Carleton re-creates and re-captures for us the rich and varied life of the Ireland he knew as a child and which vanished with the famine. In Phelim one finds the ideal and traditional folk hero, his parent's pride and the product of his upbringing. Untrammelled by social convention or an urban sense of values he is a creature as free and as audacious as Gil Blas for whom deception and intrigue are the indispensable conditions of a life lived to the full. The tale, aimed all its gaiety and vivacity of incident, testifies to a way of living as irresponsible as that set forth by Maria Edgeworth in *Castle Rackrent* at the other end of the social scale. But the manner of Carleton's recreation of it, his blending of folk-tale, fantasy and personal reminiscence into an incomparable tale makes it possible for one to feel nostalgia for a world one never even know.

'The Three Tasks', as Professor Harmon tells us in his introduction, derives more directly from the oral tradition, from a Tyrone fairytale which in turn belongs to the international folktale. The situation where a hero is faced with one or perhaps several impossible tasks at the risk of death is one of the perennial and irresistible motifs of native tradition and legend.

In 'An Essay on Irish Swearing' the tone sharpens and deepens to a caustic satire on 'the writers of the Blackwoods school who professed to find "Paddy" a compound of wit and murder, too innocent in his violence to deserve full moral censure. But it is also an angry, self-despising attack on his own people who had chosen sound rather than sense, and the rich honey of whose rhetoric could coat the most savage and degenerate of crimes.'

THE PARTY FIGHT AND FUNERAL

Volume Four

The two long stories in this volume continue and compliment the theme of Ribbonism and sectarianism treated in 'Wildgoose Lodge' (Volume 1). The atmosphere of both 'The Party Fight and Funeral' and 'Midnight Mass', clouded by the bitterness and intrigue of sectarian unrest in Irish society, is far indeed from the sunlight and firelight which gilds the world of Phelim O'Toole and his companions. These tales are a cry from the heart for an end to the madness which binds all, from the oldest to the youngest, in a vicious circle of violence, death and revenge. The evils which were so apparent to Carleton as a sworn, but sighted, Ribbonman compelled a uniquely intense and moving illumination of that society whose influence permeated every facet of the life of the people, involving now few, now many, in a ceaseless strife which ranged from gladiatorial combat to mass murder. A parallel has been drawn between this endemic violence, without cause and apparently without cure, and that which raged among the Montagues and Capulets several centuries before. The reader of Carleton today may find a present parallel in our own country for there is a chilling familiarity in his account of 'little boys at school who mimic the madness of the adults and even succeed in planning their battles on the same day fathers clash.'

Send us your name and address if you would like to receive our complete catalogue of books of Irish Interest

THE MERCIER PRESS
4 Bridge Street, Cork, Ireland